D0630669

Lovetorn

KAVITA DASWANI

An Imprint of HarperCollinsPublishers

HarperTeen is an imprint of HarperCollins Publishers.

Library of Congress Cataloging-in-Publication Data
Daswani, Kavita, date.
    Lovetorn / by Kavita Daswani. — 1st ed.
    p. cm.
    ISBN 978-0-06-167311-5 (trade bdg.)
    [1. Moving, Household—Fiction. 2. East Indians—California—Fiction. 3. Love—
Fiction. 4. Arranged marriage—Fiction. 5. Family life—California—Fiction. 6. Los
Angeles (Calif.)—Fiction.] I. Title.
PZ7.D2597Lov 2012   2011019361
[Fic]—dc23   CIP
                                                                             AC

Typography by Michelle Gengaro-Kokmen
12 13 14 15 16   LP/RRDH   10 9 8 7 6 5 4 3 2 1
❖
First Edition

For my husband, my Nissim,
the kindest man I have ever known
And our little boys, Jahan and Nirvan,
who understood when I couldn't come out to play

Acknowledgments

Thanks to my agent, Jodie Rhodes, who has about the sharpest instincts of anyone I know.

Thanks to my editor, Phoebe Yeh, and associate editor, Jayne Carapezzi, at HarperCollins, who nurtured this like it was their own and always knew I had more—and better—in me.

I am so grateful to my cousin Divya Vaswani in Bangalore, who read the earliest draft and confirmed to me that girls like Shalini were real.

Thanks to Abbey Coolidge, my link to the land of teens, who took me to her high school and told me when Shalini and her friends were "too polite."

And thanks to my dear friend, Meena Makhijani—a doctor, a dancer, and an embodiment of all that is wondrous about Indian womanhood.

One

IN A CARVED WOODEN FRAME on my mother's bedside table sits a photograph of me taken on the day that
I got engaged. I was dressed all in white, layers of stiff
tulle peeking through my skirt, a pink satin sash askew
around my waist. My thick hair had been cut short so
that the top of it stuck up stubbornly, disappearing
under part of the frame. I had tiny gold studs in my ears.
I was looking directly into the camera, a toothy smile on
my face conveying the exhausted glee that accompanies
the final moments of a three-year-old's birthday party.
My birthday party.

That image popped into my mind now, and I wondered if my mother had packed the photo in one of the
two suitcases she had been allotted by my father for this

trip. Sitting in the back of a car as we were driven away from Los Angeles International Airport to our new home on the outskirts of the city, I turned to ask her. But I thought better of it when I saw how sullen she looked. On the other side of me, my younger sister had dozed off, whistling gently through her nostrils. I slid down in the leather seat and rested my head against my mother's shoulder, turning slightly to take in the scenes whizzing past our window: the fast-food restaurants on almost every corner, the gas stations, the small shops advertising liquor and phone cards and lottery tickets. Long, immaculate highways stretched overhead, seeming to arch into the light blue sky. It was a brilliant, beautiful day.

I should have been utterly exhilarated. A sense of delight and wonder should have been coursing through my body. This was my first time in America, the only trip I had ever taken outside of my homeland of India. There was a new job for my father and a brand-new school for my sister, Sangita, and me. The prospect of this second life had been so alluring to my father that he had given up everything in India for it.

My father, sitting in the passenger seat next to the driver, was reading a copy of *Newsweek* that he had carried off the plane. This was his second trip in a month. He had come to Los Angeles on his own a few weeks ago to sign a lease on a house and fill out the paperwork at our new school. He had wanted to remain in the US and have my mother and sister and me meet him here. But instead, he had flown all the way back to Bangalore last week to help us pack up and to accompany us to our new home. My mother had insisted on it. And she had been so dead set against making the move that my father convinced himself, in this one instance, that he had to do as she'd asked.

"The weather has been wonderful," my father said to us now, tucking the magazine into a bag at his feet. "It gets a little cool in the evenings, but the daytime is very pleasant." He was trying to make small talk. "I have been busy here, making sure everything is ready for you. Setting up phones, internet, cable service. Opening bank accounts. Arranging your matters at the school. The house is very nice and comfortable. I was lucky to have found something furnished. Makes everything so much easier." He had his head turned toward the three of us in the back. My mother, her arms folded in front of her, silent, stared out of the window.

We were in the back of a yellow cab driven by a man my father kept calling Mr. Phil. (We are nothing if not unfailingly polite.) On my father's first trip here, he had happened to flag him down at the airport. Since then, my father asked for him whenever he called the cab company. As he explained to us, it wasn't like Bangalore, where you could step outside your home and signal to a passing auto-rickshaw. There were no taxis available in Los Angeles without calling ahead.

"We're lucky; there isn't much traffic," said Mr. Phil. He had a shiny bald head and wore an oversize watch on a red strap. The cab smelled of pine trees. "It's usually pretty bad on a Friday, but it's early yet. Maybe another thirty minutes or so and we should be off the One-oh-One." My father nodded knowledgeably.

I turned to my mother again.

"Don't worry, Ma," I whispered, trying to infuse some cheer into my voice. "Everything will be fine."

I put my hand on top of hers. A pallid ray of late-morning sunlight flashed against the slender ruby ring I wore on the middle finger of my right hand. I closed my eyes for a second to ward off the dull ache that was beginning to close around my heart, a sadness that existed because I had left behind the boy who had given me the ring, the boy to whom I had been promised when I was a baby, the boy to whom I was engaged.

Vikram was the person of all the many, many people I had left behind whom I had already started to miss the most. Since the day I had turned three, thirteen years ago, when he was already a "big boy" at six, we had been a constant in each other's lives. We had promised to email and text and talk all the time. But he was still twelve-and-a-half hours ahead of me. He would be asleep when I was awake, and vice versa. How could we ever really connect that way? And not seeing him for two years . . . I didn't know how I would survive it.

My eyes were growing heavy now. I closed them and succumbed to sleep.

When I awoke, we were pulling up outside our new home. My father had shown us pictures of it when he had returned to Bangalore to bring us here. He had been so excited. Now, looking at it through the window, I realized that this house at 21723 Fillmore Lane was almost identical to just about every other house on this quiet street. It was a pale beige color with a white door and a dark red tile roof. It looked like the houses I had seen in American cartoons when I was younger, where life was perfect, people were harmless, everybody was happy.

We pulled up outside. Mr. Phil helped my father get the luggage out of the trunk. I realized that this would be the first time in the course of my sixteen years that I would be entering a home where there would be nobody to greet me. My father had walked up the few steps leading to the front door and was jiggling a key in the keyhole, trying to unlock the door.

"It sometimes gets stuck," my father said a little sheepishly. "I will call the landlord to fix it."

My mother looked like she was about to erupt in fury. She didn't want to be here. She had railed hard against my father's decision—she and the rest of the large, involved family into which I had been born. It was ridiculous, she had told him. Moving thousands of miles away to a country where we didn't know a soul. It made no sense.

But my father had not listened to her. This was something he *had* to do. It was a career-making job, a once-in-a-lifetime opportunity. He wanted eventually to be like the tens of thousands of smart and upwardly mobile Indian executives working in India who referred to themselves as "America-returns." They had cachet now because they had worked in a country that was hard to emigrate to and in which it was not easy to find a good, well-paying job. But he had landed one—with a company called Indo-West Systems, a software company that he had had some dealings with in Bangalore. It was too good to pass up, even though his decision had come as such a shock to my grandfather that the two of them didn't speak for three days.

Now, waiting for my father to open the door, it was evident that my mother had already had enough. Her hands were clasped firmly in front of her, and she was muttering Hindi curse words beneath her breath. Just when she was about to say something aloud, he finally managed to turn the doorknob.

Mr. Phil gathered our things and pulled them over the threshold and into the house. We stood there, our belongings heaped around our feet. Now, finally, everything became real to me. Up until now, this talk of a "new life" had felt like a dream. But here it was, in the form of a hardwood floor entryway, a cream-carpeted dining room to one side, another room containing the largest TV I had ever seen in my life. A flight of stairs was toward the back, leading to some bedrooms upstairs. The sun was high and bright now, its rays bouncing off the brass light fixtures. Sangita excitedly grabbed my mother by her wrist and dragged her off to explore.

"Thank you for your kind courtesy once again," said my father to Mr. Phil. He reached into his wallet and pulled out a clutch of bills, which he handed to the driver. After Mr. Phil left, my father said to me, "What I gave as a tip would cover a full taxi ride in Bangalore." He laughed. I smiled weakly. My mind was elsewhere.

My father walked to a window, pulled back a blue curtain, and looked outside. It was a perfect morning. The window looked out onto the front yard, a patch of green bordered with multicolored flowers. The street was quiet and empty except for a young mother pushing a baby stroller and talking on her cell phone.

"Come, Shalini, let me show you around," my father said, holding me by my elbow. Sangita and my mother came down the stairs, my mother's face still passive and unimpressed, my sister's exuberant.

"You should come and see our rooms," Sangita gushed. *"So pretty!"* Five years younger than me, she was still a kid. She seemed the most excited to be here. She had every reason to be: she hadn't left behind the boy she loved. Thinking of Vikram left a sick feeling in my stomach now. From somewhere deep in my memory, I suddenly got a whiff of his aftershave, remembered the warmth of his eyes when he had kissed me on my forehead at the airport. I couldn't even fathom how far away he was.

"Let me see the kitchen," my mother said, her handbag still strung over her shoulder, a black sweater folded over her arms. She looked like she was ready to go somewhere instead of having just arrived.

We followed her inside, and I marveled at the clean efficiency of it all. The refrigerator was built into the wall so it seemed to take up almost no space. The stove had no food-stained gas rings; instead, it was covered with what looked like some high-tech touch pad. My mother opened a dark-wood cabinet and ran her fingers down a stack of glossy black plates, matching bowls nestled next to them. She picked up one of the clear drinking glasses and peered at it. She made her way over to the refrigerator and opened it. It was empty. She turned to my father.

"What will we do for food? There is nothing here!" she said. "Thank the Lord I packed some *dals*, some *masalas*. But still, I need onion, garlic, the basics. How can we walk into an empty house?" She was almost hysterical now, her eyes wide, her voice panic-stricken. I knew how she felt. Even though everything was so nice, so new, there was a coldness here. I missed the background noise I had grown up with, the constant chatter and hum of a house full of aunts, uncles, cousins, and grandparents.

"Asha, don't worry," my father said soothingly. "There is a very big supermarket down the road. I didn't want to leave perishables to spoil. We will go out soon, get what we need. It is a small thing."

My mother turned around and marched upstairs, the sweater still covering her forearms, the brown bag swinging from her stiff shoulders.

Two

WHILE THE REST OF US NAPPED in the afternoon, my father went out to buy groceries. In the evening, my mother prepared a salad using bagged, prewashed vegetables, followed by canned cream of mushroom soup, buttered toast, and sliced cheese. It wasn't the most momentous of first meals, but the last thing my father wanted was for my mother to start roasting eggplant and peeling potatoes. He said that when she was less jet-lagged, he would take her to the nearest Indian shop to stock up on cumin seeds, coriander powder, fresh coconuts, and chickpea flour.

We sat around the dining table looking at the alien offerings in front of us, a meal scant and slight compared to what we were used to.

"It's the first time that it's just the four of us eating dinner," said Sangita. Of course it was. In my Bangalore home, there were at least a dozen of us gathered at any time. There were so many of us, we ate in shifts.

"Yes, and later it will be the first time we have had to wash our own dishes," I said. I forced a smile.

It would be the first time we would have to lock our doors at night, shutting out the strange world that lay beyond those quiet walls. Even though we were talking, the house was eerily still, with none of the babble of aunts in the background, children playing in the hallway, maids scurrying in and out of the kitchen carrying trays of hot food and scolding the kids who got in the way. I couldn't even imagine how my father had been on his own in this house for two weeks, preparing for our arrival.

"We should call Dada soon," said my father. "He will just be waking up now."

I thought of the house I had been born in, the huge rambling structure that was the most imposing bungalow on its quiet side street in Bangalore. My grandparents, Dada and Dadi, would be stirring from sleep in their airy bedroom, my grandmother slowly creaking herself into a sitting position, easing her arthritic feet into her slippers, and hobbling to the bathroom to wash. Their maid,

Meena, who had served my grandparents for the better part of forty years, would enter with a tray of steaming *chai* and a small steel bowl of chipped sugar cubes. The morning newspapers would be brought to Dada, who by now would be reclining in a wicker chair by the window, his eyes shut in grateful salutation to another day of life. At seventy-five, he gave thanks for every morning he woke up.

And then, slowly, as if silently bidden by the rousing of the heads of the household, the rest of the family would come to life: my five uncles getting up in preparation for work, my aunts helping them with their morning routines, my spinster aunt barking instructions to the cook about what to serve for breakfast. My cousins—or as we had been taught to call one another, my cousin-brothers and cousin-sisters—would be getting dressed for school, kindergarten to college. My oldest cousin-sisters still at home—the twins Geeta and Leela—who were twenty and unmarried, would be checking the homework and packing the schoolbags and lunches for the younger children and would later be attending to the duties of the household. By ten a.m. there would only be women, babies, and household staff around.

At the farewell dinner we'd had at our home the night before we left, I had stood in a corner and counted every single family member I had lived with: thirty-seven relatives and twelve helpers, including nursemaids, cooks, kitchen boys, cleaning ladies, drivers, and Vishal and Chandan, the two old men who took turns staying up at night, sitting on a round stool in front of the gate surrounding our house in a bid to provide the security that was never really needed.

I had realized then that I had never actually thought of that before, that I had simply taken for granted that there were all these people under one roof, all the relatives that I had grown up with who had given birth in the adjacent room or died a floor above or been tearfully sent away in marriage on a marigold-strewn path outside the house. It was a noisy and bustling household. It was not always happy; with thirty-seven people and four generations under one roof, how could it be? But it was a life that was busy and full and mostly loving, and there was great comfort in that. Dada had been adamant that his six sons, their wives, and the rest of the brood would live together. The only way he would agree to one of us leaving was if a) she was a daughter of the house and had been married off to a family of Dada's choosing, or b) if he or she died.

While Sangita, my mother, and I cleared the table and did the dishes, my father retreated to his downstairs office to call his parents. I heard him talking with Dada, then to a few of my uncles, recounting the details of the flight over, the weather, how my mother and sister and I were doing. It was mundane information; but, in my mind, the conversation proved that things had now finally returned to normal between my father and Dada. Just a few days earlier, when my father had come back to Bangalore to fetch us, there had been another blowup between him and Dada, my grandfather accusing his son of taking us away, my father telling him that it was just for two years, until his contract was up.

I should have been reassured. But instead, there was a fine edge to my father's voice, and a raw anger in my mother's eyes, that left me feeling unsettled.

Three

SANGITA AND I DECIDED TO SHARE A ROOM, even though there was an extra bedroom next door. We had never slept apart. In a house with thirty-seven people, space was at a premium.

The jet lag was horrible. I fell asleep at nine, woke up at midnight, tossed and turned like a dying fish out of water. Nothing would help me get back to sleep. I went downstairs at two a.m. and found my mother sitting on the couch in the den, the TV on, watching someone trying to sell cooking appliances. I sat down next to her.

"You can't even call Vikram, can you?" she asked. I shook my head. Right after seeing us off at the airport, my fiancé was going to visit his sick grandfather in a remote part of Jodhpur, staying in a house that had no phone. He said he would try and get to one of the public international calling booths in town; but with the time difference and lack of access, he might not be able to call until Monday. The timing, in my mind, couldn't have been worse. Right now I would have done anything just to hear his voice.

"We've been here less than twenty-four hours and I'm miserable," my mother said bluntly. Her eyes stared vacantly at the screen. The woman was cheerfully showing how easy it was to make soups and sauces.

"You're just jet-lagged, Ma," I said. "We all are."

"Your father isn't," she said bitterly. "He's upstairs, snoring away."

"Don't be mad at him, Ma. He wanted to do the right thing."

"Well," my mother said, standing up. "He didn't."

I fell asleep on the couch, the TV still on. When I woke up, it was eight thirty. I heard Sangita in the kitchen, my father's voice in the background. My head felt as if it was stuffed with cotton balls. I dragged myself up and went to join them.

"I didn't want to wake you, *beti*," said my father. "The first few days are hard." He was speaking like an old pro.

"Is Ma still asleep?" I asked. My father nodded, stirring sugar into hot tea.

"Come," he said. "Have something. When your mother wakes up, we will go together to the Indian store; and I will take you all around, show you the neighborhood, the mall." We were lucky enough, he said, to be within walking distance of many basic amenities; even the school Sangita and I had been enrolled in was within fifteen minutes on foot, though we could take the bus if we wanted to. My father had also started driving lessons and would soon get a car and his license. There would be no shortage of ways for us to get to school.

My mother finally came downstairs after eleven, yesterday's *kohl* streaked down her cheek, her hair a mess, her *mangalsutra*—a necklace made of black beads and gold that is worn by most married Hindu women—tangled in the lace collar of her nightgown. She didn't say a word and headed straight for the cabinet, retrieved a glass, and filled it with water from a plastic bottle on the counter. She gulped down the water thirstily and turned to go back upstairs. She hesitated for a second as if she had suddenly realized we were there, in her midst, waiting for a word from her. But it was as if the thought then disappeared. She put the glass back on the counter and left the kitchen.

Sangita and I turned to look at our father.

"She's just tired," he said.

An hour later my father knocked on their bedroom door to see if she'd like to join us, explore the neighborhood, pick up some groceries. Her initial response was to say no. He tried to open the door. It was locked. I had never known my mother to shut us out like that before. I don't even think most of the doors back home in India *had* locks.

"Asha, why have you locked yourself in?" he asked. There was silence. "Look, I'll take you to the Indian store," he said. "Delhi Delites and Supplies. Nice chap from Ludhiana runs it. I've told him all about you and the girls." Then he pressed himself to the door and lowered his voice. "Please, Asha, just come. We need some provisions for the house. I don't know what to get. I need you."

After a brief silence we heard some movement inside, the clicking of the doorknob turning. She stood in the doorway as unkempt as she had been earlier.

"Okay, fine," she said. "Give me fifteen minutes to get ready."

We waited outside the house for her, enjoying the cool midmorning breeze. From a few houses down came the sound of a radio turned on high volume, an American pop song playing a peppy, cheerful tune. Across the street a man in green shorts was hosing down his car while his young son rode up and down the sidewalk on a tricycle. This scene, right here, captured everything I knew to be American.

I drew in a deep breath. I calculated the time in India and imagined what Vikram was doing at that moment. He would be lying alone in the room next to his grandfather's, covered by a woolen blanket, a small lamp by his bed shining onto the pages of the fantasy novel he had started just before I'd left. He had said that reading would help distract him from thoughts of me. I had smiled and rubbed his cheek. Thinking about this, I remembered the scent of his cologne, how his chin felt when he hadn't shaved for a few days. He would nuzzle my forehead, one arm clasped around my shoulders, a show of affection when nobody was looking. A small sob caught in my throat now as I let those thoughts of him wash over me.

My mother finally appeared, wrapped in an embroidered gray shawl.

"How are we going?" she asked. "Where is the taxi?"

My father smiled broadly.

"No need for Mr. Phil today," he said. "We will walk,

then take a bus. You will enjoy it."

Sangita linked her arm through my mother's and carried her bag. Her two slender braids swung behind her as she walked. Usually my mother braided both my hair and my sister's. Today I had done my own and helped Sangita with hers.

My father led us down the wide, clean street. For us this was like another world. No potholes and *paan*-stained pavements, no mangy dogs blocking our path. No relentless honking of cars and auto-rickshaws, no running the risk of being knocked over by a bicyclist carrying bales of fabric. There were no hawkers selling raw bananas and used books blocking the path. It was seamless, organized.

"This is the local coffee place," my father said, leading us into a long stretch of stores. There was a Starbucks, a massive grocery store, a mailbox rental place, somewhere to buy *shawarmas* and sandwiches, a drugstore on the far end. Everything was brightly lit and bustling: cars pulling in and out of the parking lot, people clutching the hands of their kids. It felt safe and sanitized. My father took my mother just inside the automatic doors of the big supermarket so she could get a sense of the size of it. She gazed at the high ceilings, the rows and rows of shelves piled with things she had never seen before. By the entrance, she picked up an orange, smelled it, and put it back.

"This store has everything," my father said. He was speaking with the pride of someone who may have built it

We continued walking, rounding a corner. My father pointed to the opposite side of the street, at an imposing pair of brick buildings, one smaller and set farther back than the other. Valley Crest Middle and High School. From Monday on, Sangita and I would be going here, to the local public school.

"I chose our new home because of its proximity to this school, which I believe to be an excellent one," he said. "It offers a fine standard of education." My father often lapsed into this formal mode of speech with us when he felt marginally nervous about something. I could tell by his expression that he so badly wanted Sangita and me to like what we were seeing.

"It looks nice, Papa," I said, trying to hide my nervousness. Compared to the small convent school I had attended in Bangalore, this new place was vast, intimidating. I couldn't wait to get away from it.

"Where to next, Papa?" I asked.

We retraced our steps, took a small side street lined with pretty houses that ended up on another main road.

21

At the corner there was a bus stop. Within a few minutes, a bright orange bus trundled along, and the four of us boarded. Fifteen minutes later, we arrived at our destination. We walked past a gas station selling one-dollar hot dogs, a rundown shop filled with party favors and plastic toys, a place offering thirty flavors of frozen yogurt. As soon as we opened the door to Delhi Delites and Supplies, the jaunty, popular Bollywood music reached my ears, the scent of rose essence and curry powder tickled my nose. I felt every muscle in my body relax. It felt like home.

"*Bhai sahib*, at last you have brought the family!" shouted out a chubby, bearded man in a blue turban who was rearranging shelves next to the entrance, addressing my father like a brother. He came over and shook my father's hand. Then he folded his hands in greeting toward my mother and sister and me.

"This is Mr. Ranjit Singh, the proprietor," said my father. Mr. Singh slapped my father jovially on the back.

"This man has been lonely without his family here, coming in to eat alone," said Mr. Singh. My heart broke a little, imagining my father by himself, sitting at a table for one, eating the foods of his homeland.

We walked into the cafeteria part of the store, which

was slowly filling up with hungry families. While my father ordered, my mother roamed the aisles with a red plastic basket strung over her arm, sniffing packets of coriander powder and examining green chilies and onions up close before placing them in little bags. Like me, she too was at home here.

On Monday morning Sangita and I woke up early to get ready for school. It was late September, a few weeks after the new school year had started. Sangita was going into sixth grade, me into high school. I had a nervous ache in my stomach. I had been here three days and still hadn't spoken to Vikram. I so desperately needed to hear his voice now, to hear him tell me everything would be okay. He always knew the right thing to say.

As my sister showered, I sat cross-legged on my bed. A quiet panic had come over me. Ever since kindergarten, and right up until the day I left India, I had had the same group of friends. Two of my cousin-sisters were part of that group. I knew that every day when I got to school, I would automatically have my friends there, girls with whom I could instantly chatter and giggle. It was like going to a family reunion, and I had loved it. But here it was going to be just me, my younger sister in an adjacent building. I had never been friends with anyone who wasn't Indian. American girls were, in my mind, a different breed completely. I couldn't imagine what we would have in common.

The panic intensified. This was too much, too soon. We had only had a few days in this country. It was too rushed. We needed more time. I stood up to go tell my parents. But then the bathroom door opened, and Sangita was standing in the doorway, her cheeks still warm from the hot shower, buttoning up her blouse.

"This is so exciting, no, *didi*?" she said, calling me "big sister." "A new school, new friends. It's so *grreeat*." Her childlike enthusiasm touched me. I wished I could feel some of it. She saw the anxious look on my face. "What's the matter, *didi*? Are you not feeling well? I know it was hard to sleep last night because of the jet lag. But maybe we can rest when we come home. It's going to be really fun, our first day of school. Aren't you looking forward to it?"

I took her hand and held it, looking at her sweet, expectant, bespectacled face.

"Yes, yes, of course I'm looking forward to it," I lied. "Come now, let's eat some breakfast quickly and go."

A short while later we stood at the door, Sangita and I both in our "best frocks"—in India, those dresses had been reserved for special family gatherings. They

24

were both the same style, but in different colors: mine in black-and-white, Sangita's in blue-and-pink. Each dress consisted of a blouse and skirt that had been sewn together, banded at the waist with a belt. The shirt had an eyelet collar, pearl buttons down the front, and long sleeves. The skirts came down below our knees. We were both wearing skin-colored panty hose through which, if you looked closely enough, you could see the hair on our legs flattened against our skin. Our shoes, bought just for this trip, were identical, black leather with small heels, silver buckles on the front.

My mother appeared from the kitchen holding a small silver tray with a devotional flame at its center. She came toward us and circled the tray around the both of us, uttering a Sanskrit prayer beneath her breath to bless us on the start of a new journey. She did not, I noticed, perform the same ritual on my father, who was already waiting for us outside the house, ready to walk us to school before being picked up there by Mr. Phil, who would drive him to work. She handed us each a small tin lunch box, gave us a quick, watery kiss good-bye, and shut the door.

Our father carried our school bags, containing basic stationery supplies and our lunch boxes, walking two steps ahead of us as if anxious to get somewhere, to start his day. He said, "You girls will be getting the very best education here, very superior quality. Please, girls, you don't worry about anything. You will make friends and be excellent in your studies, yes?" It was his stab at a pep talk, something to cheer us up.

Our thick, formal shoes clunked heavily against the pavement, the polyester of our pleated skirts swished gently against our legs until we arrived right outside the school. A row of yellow school buses were empty-ing out, and people were dropping off their kids, kissing them good-bye; the younger ones moving through the main entrance to the building in the back. The students were a mass of denim jeans, colorful T-shirts, backpacks adorned with dangling charms, sweatshirts tied around waists. Sneakers in a myriad of different colors, boots lined with fur. Some of the boys lightly knocked their knuckles together, an odd greeting ritual I had never seen before. Everything seemed casual and carefree.

I looked down at my dress and instantly felt out of place, as if I were ready to go to my grandma's birthday party instead of coming to my first day in a Los Angeles school. Looking at all of the casually dressed students around me, I suddenly craved the security of a school uniform, the red-and-gray-checked dresses we all wore at my old school that made us all equal, none prettier or richer than the others. Here, now, I had never felt more out of place.

My father led us through the main entrance and down a corridor lined with room after room after room, with kids rushing about everywhere. I couldn't imagine ever being a part of this world, ever getting to the point where I would belong.

The principal's office was at the far end of the corridor. Her secretary took our names before knocking on the principal's open door to tell her that we were here. Mrs. Meyers was like no school head I had ever seen. My old headmistress in Bangalore was a plump and bespectacled woman who was always clad in a sari and sporting a huge red *bindi*, a dot in the middle of her forehead. But Mrs. Meyers looked young, was very thin, and had a pleasant smile on her lightly freckled face. She wore an orange shirt tucked into a fitted gray skirt.

"Welcome," she said, looking at Sangita and me. We didn't sit down. She told me that my transcripts from my old school indicated that I should be in the advanced math class, but that as she had explained to my father, the class was full for now. Perhaps when a spot opened up. She would have someone take me to my homeroom, someone else escort Sangita to where the sixth-grade classes were. She was sure we'd get caught up in no time. She wasted no words.

We all nodded silently, three black, bobbing heads in front of her desk.

"Mr. Agarwal," she said, turning to my father. "Encourage your girls to get involved with all aspects of school. There are plenty of extracurricular programs."

She asked her assistant to hand over our schedules, indicating that our conversation was over.

My father turned to leave but stopped. He gave my sister and me a quick hug—something he had never done before. "Thank you, my girls. Thank you." And just as I thought I saw a tiny tear at the corner of his right eye, he turned and walked out.

four

A FEW MINUTES LATER, halfway down the corridor, I lost Sangita. A woman who had been summoned to Mrs. Meyers's office took my sister and spirited her off in another direction. Sangita didn't even turn around to wave good-bye to me; instead, she briskly trotted alongside her escort. Another woman walked me up a flight of stairs to get to my homeroom.

It was bigger and more crowded than I had expected. The rest of the students were seated and looked up at me when I walked in. There was a murmur among some of them, giggling among others. Two girls in the third row nudged each other and pointed to my dress, chuckling into their hands. One wore a T-shirt with a glittery peace logo on the front. The other had three earrings studding her left ear.

I knew they were making fun of me. I felt the heat rise to my cheeks. I squirmed imperceptibly. I hadn't been here for thirty seconds and was already miserable. I hated it and wanted to turn around, run out the door and back down the stairs, and catch up with my father and beg him to take me home—not the new one here but our real home, the one nine thousand miles away, the one we never should have left.

"Hello, Shalini, I'm Mr. White, your homeroom and English lit teacher," said a youngish-looking man in an open-necked checked shirt and brown pants, his laptop open on the desk. He turned to the room and introduced me. "This is Shalini Agarwal, everyone. She and her family just arrived from India. Let's welcome her."

I stood there feeling self-conscious, aware of all the eyes skimming every inch of me as if I were naked.

"Why don't you take one of the empty seats in the back?" Mr. White said. I was relieved. Right then, I wanted to be nowhere else but in the background. He exchanged a few quick words with the woman who had accompanied me, and she quietly left the room.

I walked down the aisle, still feeling everyone watching me, and found the farthest desk in the farthest corner. From my black leather bag I pulled out a red tin pencil case and a brand-new lined notebook, its pages crisp and smelling faintly of petroleum. As Mr. White made various school-related announcements, I flipped over my notebook to the final page onto which I had glued a picture of Vikram and myself taken a couple of months ago.

We had gone to the Lalbagh Botanical Garden, one of Bangalore's most beautiful and ancient gardens and a favorite place of ours. Our families had accompanied us; at our age we were still too young to go off anywhere by ourselves, although my father had said that that would change when I turned eighteen, right before we got married. The picture had been taken in the Rose Garden, the heart and soul of Lalbagh, where one could find a hundred and fifty varieties of roses, although Vikram used to joke that they all looked the same to him.

I stared now at the photo: Vikram sitting cross-legged on the ground wearing a white T-shirt with a small green crocodile on the pocket and blue jeans; me standing above him dressed in a pink cotton *kurta* and pants. I had one hand on each of his shoulders and was beaming happily. We could have been cousins, brother and sister, best friends, two teenagers out at the park on a sunny Sunday. I put my finger on the photo and, with the tip of my nail, traced the outline of his face.

And now, sitting in the back of this classroom with thirty people I had never before seen and with whom I would never be friends, my heart ached for him.

I turned my attention back to Mr. White. On the blackboard behind him was written *Beowulf*, and around that a list of themes connected to the poem. I felt the smallest flutter of comfort; I had just been studying it in school in India.

Mr. White made his way to my desk and gave me his copy of the book.

"Do you know this?" Mr. White asked me once he was back at his desk. I stood up as I had been taught to do at school in India when being addressed by a teacher.

"Yes, sir," I said. "I had in fact just been studying the same before coming here. I had been writing a paper on heroic concepts as perceived in the poem, sir." In the quiet of the room, my accent sounded jarring even to me. I heard twittering and more giggles. The two girls who had laughed at me when I came in were now loudly imitating my accent.

Mr. White looked over at them sternly. "Sasha, Magali," he said. "That's enough." I wasn't sure what was worse: being teased or having to be defended by a teacher within my first five minutes of being here. Mr.

White turned back to me, his eyes sympathetic.

"Thanks for your input, Shalini," he said. "You can sit down now."

At the end of the class, Mr. White asked me to stay behind for a minute.

"I just wanted to officially welcome you," he said, gathering his papers and putting them into a gray satchel. "How do you like everything so far?"

"I have just arrived from Bangalore on Friday, sir," I said. "Everything is still new."

"Well, at least you're interested in great literature. So as far as I'm concerned, you'll do well in my class." He smiled at me, and I felt a little heartened.

"Thank you, sir," I said. "I hope so." I turned to leave, but Mr. White summoned me back.

"Oh, and Shalini. There's really no need to stand up every time a teacher talks to you." He grinned. "It just makes everyone else look bad."

Outside the classroom, I looked at the schedule. Mathematics next, followed by art. Then lunch and more classes. I wondered how Sangita was doing, where she was. I looked out a window toward the wide pathway that connected the building I was in to where she was, as if it were the one remaining artery keeping me alive. In all this strangeness, I surprised myself with how much I needed my eleven-year-old sister by my side.

The hallways were crowded. I had no idea where the next room was, so I summoned up the courage to ask a girl passing by. She didn't make fun of me, barely even noticed me. She gave me directions, and I made my way to the classroom. Mathematics was easy; the teacher—a short bespectacled man named Mr. Jeffries—handed me a worksheet to complete so he could see where I was academically, leaving me grateful for the opportunity to sit quietly and work without having to engage with anyone.

After Art, I managed to find the cafeteria, which could be accessed by the students of both schools, although it seemed that there was barely any crossover. But finally, at lunchtime, Sangita found me there. She came rushing up to me.

"*Didi*, how was it?" she asked, her eyes opened wide. "How were your classes?"

"Okay," I said, balancing a tray on which wobbled a solitary bottle of water. "Come, let's go sit somewhere."

"I already ate," she said. "But I'll sit with you."

We found a table. I fished out the lunch my mother had packed. It was made up of three small containers linked together by a wide clasp. Sangita's was identical, differentiated only by a sticker of silvery pink wings on hers and a shiny red heart on mine.

I carefully unclasped the first container. There was white rice dotted with mushy green peas, faintly scented of cloves and cinnamon. Underneath that was shredded cabbage fried in oil with green chilies. And in the final one, yogurt whipped with water until it was a creamy liquid, garnished with cilantro and flavored with salt and paprika.

"How was your morning?" I asked Sangita. "Did you enjoy your classes?"

"We did a cool science project," she said, her voice sounding enthusiastic. "We were experimenting with static electricity. I had a partner, a nice girl named Amy." Sangita began scanning the area for her new friend. She talked excitedly about her experiments. I wanted to listen but found myself distracted, wondering at how she seemed to have had such a pleasant morning while mine was not. Nobody had teased or made fun of her, and I hated the fact that this made me feel more alone.

"Hey, you," said a voice from a table behind us. I turned around and recognized a boy, Charlie, from homeroom. He had spiky hair and was wearing a faded black T-shirt that looked like it had been washed too many times. He was sitting with two other boys.

"What crap do you have in there?" he asked, pointing

to my lunch. "It's stinking the place up." His eyes were narrowed. The boys with him stared at me.

Heat rushed to my face, a cold fear clutching my heart. Sangita opened her mouth to say something, but I shook my head at her. She remained silent.

"So what happened? All the call center jobs were taken, and you had to come here?" Charlie said. A boy with him laughed. "You know, my dad lost his job 'cuz it was outsourced. One of you people must have taken it." His voice was menacing.

I was suddenly scared. Sangita put her hand on top of mine. Tears stung my eyes. My mind raced frantically to think of something to say. But nothing came to mind. I was trembling and humiliated and speechless.

"Dude, leave 'em alone," his friend said, nudging Charlie with his elbow.

With that the three boys picked up their trays and walked away. Charlie glared at me over his shoulder as he left.

Sangita looked at me, our hands still clasped together. We finished eating in silence. Her break ended before my lunchtime was over. When she had to leave, I remained there, my shoulders hunched over, tears dripping into my mother's food.

Science and Social Studies still to go. I didn't know

how I would get through the rest of the day. I was terrified that Charlie would be in one of my next classes. I couldn't face him again.

In Science I was distracted and jumpy, looking up at the door every time someone walked up and unable to concentrate on carbon compounds.

As I walked to Social Studies, I kept looking over my shoulder, convinced that Charlie was trailing me. In the class, led by an Armenian teacher, we read about the rise of industrialization and how it changed the face of early America. The teacher, Ms. Jalashgar, was animated and fun, and I could see that the other students liked her. Part of me would have loved to listen fully, to learn. But all I could think about was how little I wanted to be here, that America was the last place in the world I would have chosen to come to.

I had never been so happy to see my father, who was waiting outside the school at three that afternoon to take us home. He was leaning on the door of Mr. Phil's taxi.

"Come, girls, you must be tired," my father said jovially. "It's a short drive home."

My first day had gone worse than I could ever have imagined. I hated the fact that I was teased and had ended the day as friendless as when I'd begun it. I just wanted to get away from school and never come back.

"How was it?" my father asked once Sangita and I were settled in the back. My satchel sat heavily on my lap, weighed down with textbooks and papers. My new black shoes pinched my toes. I felt suffocated.

"It was okay, Papa," I volunteered. Mr. Phil looked at me through his rearview mirror.

"And you, *beta*?" he asked of Sangita.

"Actually, Papa, it was fun. It's a good school. They have a lot of cool things. I met a nice girl, Amy. She was my science experiment partner." The more Sangita spoke, the worse I felt. My father turned to me again, a look of worry crossing his face.

"Sangita, it seems like you are settling in. Shalini, tell me," he asked. He wanted more details from me, but I wasn't prepared to give them to him. If I started talking about the awful things Charlie had said to me or the way Sasha had referred to me as "Miss al-Qaeda" as I walked past her locker this afternoon, I would start to cry.

"Papa, don't worry. Everything was okay. We will adjust," I said.

"Tomorrow will be a better day," he said finally. "Every day will be easier. Before long you will be telling me you are loving it here."

* * *

We rode the rest of the way in silence.

At home I went upstairs to change. I stopped in the doorway of the bedroom that was to have been Sangita's. My mother had transformed it into a makeshift temple. She had brought everything to replicate the daily prayer ceremonies of our home in India. A low dresser was overlaid with one of her saris: a flowing blue-and-gold fabric that smelled of her. Over it she had placed a dozen figurines of Hindu deities: the gods Ganesha, Vishnu, and Shiva; the goddesses Parvati, Laxmi, and Durga.

In the center was a tall statue of the blue-skinned Krishna, his baby face framed by bouncy black porcelain curls, his rose petal lips curled around his flute, his most potent instrument, intoxicating all who heard it, bringing *gopis*—maidens—to their soft-skinned knees. Here, in this otherwise plain room, the golden flute on the statue stood out like a beacon.

I stepped inside and stood in front of the shrine. The stone figure of Durga was painted in bright, garish colors. She was sitting atop a tiger, her eyes wild, her ten arms carrying a myriad of weapons. Under her golden, gem-studded crown her hair was long and loose. I realized now, staring at her, that I had never really looked at her before, that this statue—like so many I had grown up with in our home temple in India—was just another piece of carved and decorated stone that I had bowed to every morning. I realized I hadn't prayed since we had left India. Given the way I was feeling now, empty and lonely, it seemed a good time. I looked straight into Durga's wide eyes, folded my hands together, bowed my head, and said a prayer that tomorrow would be a better day at school.

five

ALTHOUGH MY FATHER'S BOSS, Mr. Jairam Thakker, was Indian, he liked to be called Jeremy. Jeremy Tucker. Or as Sangita and I would refer to him, Mr. Jeremy.

My father was talking enthusiastically about him, his smarts, his vision, his drive. Work was going great, my father said. This was really the right move.

We were sitting around the coffee table in the living room after dinner. Sangita was peering intently at a new needlepoint project, and my mother was reading the Hindi newspaper she had picked up from the Indian store the other day. I was on the floor, wrapped in a pink crocheted blanket, its tiny frayed threads brushing against my cheek. On my father's iPod was a recording of a golden oldie, a song by Kishore Kumar, who was

41

known for his sad, melancholic ballads. I wished that we could be listening to something a bit more cheerful, perhaps one of the new hip-hop–inspired Hindi tunes that were all the rage in India. But now, with these soulful songs playing in the background, I was overcome by homesickness, something that took me a few minutes to define because I had never felt it before. In the still quiet of the night, with only the occasional sound of a car whooshing by outside, I longed profoundly to be back at a house where two sleepy old men stood guard outside beneath a dusky sky, chewing betel leaves wrapped around areca nuts and gossiping about the neighbors.

My father hadn't had much of a chance to talk about his new job before this. Everything had happened so fast: the offer, the plans, the departure. He had flown to Los Angeles, gotten everything set up, flown back to bring us. In all the chaos of the transition, we hadn't had a chance to hear anything about this man who had changed our lives, who had taken me away from a boy who had loved me since I was an infant. Jeremy Tucker helped big companies plan technology, had needed someone skilled in Core Java and J2EE middleware. And in hiring my father, he had wrested me away from the life I had known. My father was the only one of six brothers not to be in my grandfather's textile business.

The only way Dada and my father had come to any sort of peace over the departure was because my father had promised to return to India when this was all over in a couple of years.

"Was it a good day for you, Papa?" I asked now, resting my head on my shoulder. "Do you like it there?"

"Yes," he said, his eyes shining. "I will be working with a new client, an important insurance company. I am confident things will go well. Really, I am very lucky to be here."

My mother let out a little grunt and went back to her newspaper.

Apart from the music, it was quiet for a moment. It was morning in India. Vikram would soon be on his way home from his grandfather's. He'd be calling me in the morning. I could predict his actions like clockwork.

"Papa, tell me again," I said, breaking the silence.

"Tell you what, *beta*?" he asked.

"About the day that everything happened. With Vikram. My third birthday."

My father sighed deeply. I'd heard the story a hundred times but never tired of it. And I needed to hear it right now, like a newborn needs to nurse at a second's notice. I needed the comfort, the distraction. The details were etched in my mind: how my father had been best friends with Vikram's father, Uncle Bhushan, for thirty years—from boyhood. They'd met when they were ten, two scrawny and bespectacled boys sitting on top of the brick wall that stood between their homes tossing tiny pebbles into the street. That wall was the only thing that stood between them. They had crammed for exams together; and when my father had his first college crush, Bhushan had been the only person he had told. During religious festivals, my father would finish family prayers at home and then climb over the wall to Bhushan's house. They had gotten married within eleven days of each other. Uncle Bhushan and his wife, Aunty Bharati, had their first child—my Vikram—within a year. I had come along three years later. At my Namkaran—naming ceremony—when the priest whispered *Shalini* in my ear, thus giving me my name, Vikram had held my tiny fingers in his pudgy hand. Forty days after I was born, when there was the customary ceremony before my mother was allowed to take me out of the house for the first time, we had gone to visit Uncle Bhushan and Aunty Bharati. They had moved an hour away by then; but my father likes to tell me that, after crying in the car the entire trip, once I'd heard Vikram's voice, I had been instantly soothed.

"That was something, the day of your third birthday,"

my father said now, a look of nostalgia crossing his face. I pulled the blanket tighter around me. "Fifty children playing inside the house. It was crazy. I went outside to the garden for some peace and quiet. Bhushan was sitting there, in the same white wooden chair we still have. He was drinking Limca. Then out you came, crying because the pink icing from your cake was all over your pretty white lace dress."

I laughed a little now. This was my favorite part.

"Vikram put a handkerchief to his mouth," my father continued. "He licked it and tried to wipe the stain off your dress, telling you, 'Na roh, don't cry.' You stopped immediately. He took your hand and led you back to the party. It was then that Bhushan turned to me and suggested it, that we should pledge you two to be together in marriage. I was very surprised. Even in our tradition, it rarely happens like this anymore, when two people are so young. But it made sense. It would have happened anyway. Vikram's father and I simply decided to take matters into our own hands."

I smiled. To me it was the most glorious fairy tale.

Suddenly, my mother put down her newspaper. "Well, I didn't think it was the best of ideas," she said sternly. I sat up straight. She had never told me this before.

"On that day I told your father, 'Girish, what are you

thinking? They are just children. Maybe they are friends now; but who knows what they will be in ten or twenty years, where their lives will take them, what fate has in store?'"

My father was quiet. Sangita looked up from the bare-bones beginning of her tapestry.

"Don't misunderstand me, Shalini," my mother said. "I love that family. Vikram is like my son. I just didn't think we had the right to make that decision for you. But I had no choice. I had to accept it. The men had decided." She stared at me for a second. There was an emptiness in her eyes.

"Look at you now," she said. "Your heart is breaking because you are so far away from him. It is not fair to put you through this."

"Asha, no need to be so dramatic," my father said, brushing away my mother's fears now just as he no doubt must have done thirteen years earlier. He stood up and stretched. "The children are strong. They will survive.

"And, Shalini," he said, turning to me. "Please don't feel sad. You and Vikram are destined to be together. It is written in the stars. In the meantime, there is always Skype."

Six

THE PHONE RANG very early the next morning. I jumped out of bed and rushed downstairs to answer it, knowing it would be him. My Vikram.

"Hi, Shalu," a boy's voice said gently. I felt a little flip in my belly. "How are you? How was the flight?" he asked. His soft, steady voice made my heart hum. I pressed my lips close to the receiver.

"It was okay." I paused. Tears flooded my eyes now. "I really miss you," I sobbed. Talking to Vikram for the first time since I got here drove home the fact that I was so far away from him. I clutched the phone tightly, afraid to drop it as if doing so would sever my connection to him. I thought back to the last time I was with him, at the airport. Thousands of people surrounded us, but for those few moments it had seemed as if it was just he and I alone in that large, chaotic space. Our hands had touched. He had wanted to kiss me, but that was something not done in public in my culture, especially not between two teenagers. Tears had streamed down my face. He had wiped them away, the way he had done since I was a little girl.

"What if you forget me, Vikram?" I had asked him.

"As if you'll let me!" he'd joked. "And it's you who might forget me, being in exciting America. Maybe you won't want to return."

"That will never happen," I had said. "Never." I had looked down at the ruby ring he had given me, an identical one on his finger. We had exchanged them a few days earlier in front of a shrine at Vikram's house. His mother had insisted on it, said it was "high time." I remember my mother being quiet, withdrawn from the proceedings.

Now I pressed the phone hard against my ear.

"I miss everything," I said. "This place is so different. Everything is so new. I don't like it. My school is horrible."

"It's only been a few days," he soothed. "Give it time. You will find friends; you will get used to it. You'll see."

I nodded silently. He told me he loved me. I wiped

the tears from my eyes and hung up. My mother was standing behind me.

"Vikram?" she asked. I nodded. My bottom lip trembled. I expected her to come toward me and comfort me the way she always did. But she shook her head, turned around, walked into the kitchen, put the kettle on for me.

I went upstairs to get ready. I put the stiff dress and panty hose I'd worn yesterday in the back of my closet and pulled out a pair of denim jeans—still new, crisp, and dark blue—a simple cotton tunic shirt, and a pair of flat leather sandals. I peered into the mirror, ran my tongue self-consciously over my braces, and tucked a few stray wisps of hair back into my braid. Sangita came out of the bathroom, showered and dressed, in a pair of khakis and a plain red T-shirt. She looked much more comfortable than I felt. Around her wrist were prayer beads, wound trendily. With her still-damp hair left loose and falling over one eye, a thin black cord around her neck, she looked almost American. She looked like one of them.

Outside school a short while later, I stood, frozen. It was harder today than it had been the previous day, when I hadn't known what to expect. Here, now, I was filled with dread at being teased again, at having people laugh and whisper behind my back, at feeling left out of everything.

"Come, *didi*," Sangita said, pulling me by the hand. "We'll be late. Let's go." I wished I had even a fraction of her enthusiasm. I tentatively let her lead me inside.

In English class I settled into my seat, lifted my book bag, and pulled out the copy of *Beowulf* that Mr. White had given me. Charlie, the mean boy from the cafeteria yesterday, turned to me and grimaced, as if my mere presence had completely ruined his day. I tried to block him out, to forget he was even there, and concentrate on my lesson.

I was relieved when the bell finally sounded. I started packing up my things. I looked up and noticed two girls walking toward me. Sasha was the pretty blond one and Magali beautiful and black, with a mass of dark ringlets, but both memorable to me only because of their meanness. They were both slender and petite, and wore the low-waist jeans that seemed to be the favorite look at this school, held in place with thick belts. Magali's pants had a tear near the knee, although it looked as if it had been put there on purpose; and Sasha's golden hair was even shinier against a turquoise scarf around her neck that appeared to have been made from confetti. I had a nervous smile on my face. But they were approaching me, looking friendly. They were probably coming up to say hello and to ask if I needed anything. Maybe they would befriend me, like Amy had done with Sangita. Perhaps things wouldn't be so bad after all, just like Vikram had predicted.

They were both standing right in front of me now. I beamed up at them, about to stand up and shake their hands.

"Here," Sasha said, dropping a small white-and-orange box on my desk. "You could probably use this." She and Magali snickered and walked off. I picked up the box. It said on the top, CREAM HAIR REMOVER FOR THE FACE—FAST, LASTING RESULTS.

I glanced up and saw Sasha and Magali standing by the door, both staring straight at me, huddling close to each other and laughing. My whole body had suddenly become ten degrees hotter. I put the box in my bag, waited until they had left the doorway, and then made my way out. I spent the rest of the day praying I wouldn't see them again.

Sangita met me on the steps at the end of the afternoon. She was chatting amiably with a red-haired girl.

"Hi, *didi*," she said. "This is my friend Amy."

The girl waved at me casually.

"Hey," she said. She had an open and friendly face, a

gap-toothed smile. She wore her hair in a high ponytail, which swung from side to side as she talked.

"I gotta walk down the block to meet my mom," she said to Sangita. "Call me later, okay?" She lightly touched my sister's hand, gave her a bright smile, and bounced down the rest of the steps.

"She's nice, right?" my sister said, turning back to me. "She introduced me to her other friends, Kayla and Beth. They are also really nice. Beth is Chinese. She was adopted by an American family. I never met anyone adopted before." Sangita was excited and happy.

"How was your second day, *didi*?" she asked. "Do you feel better about being here?"

I nodded brusquely and shoved my hand into my open bag, pushing down the box of hair cream before Sangita saw it.

Seven

BEFORE LEAVING BANGALORE, I had bought a small pink diary, its front cover decorated with a picture of a climbing vine. I had never had a diary before; but in view of the life change that loomed before me, I thought it might be a good idea to have a place to record my thoughts and feelings. It was also a way for me to remember all the things I wanted to tell Vikram. I had had no need of such a thing before, as he and I would talk many times a day and saw each other all the time; and he would happily listen to even the most mundane details of my life.

But with an ocean and a large time difference between us, I knew that wouldn't be so easy anymore. Even though we could email back and forth, I would miss not hearing his voice several times a day.

Now, however, that diary served a whole other purpose. On the day we arrived, I had started instead to make a list of all the firsts I had experienced in that one day alone: the quietness of the house, the cheese sandwich for dinner, the fact that I could watch anything I wanted on TV without fearing that Dada would come in any minute and change channels.

In the two weeks that we had been here, I had filled four pages of the diary with all these firsts—things as inconsequential as having the electrician show up at precisely the appointed time, which never happens in India. The diary had become my best friend, my confidante, the replacement for all I had left behind. It had become something that was just for me.

Some of the entries on my list were repeats: I had listed Doritos at least three times, because I just really loved them. And some were meaningless: next to "Kiwi Strawberry Snapple" I had written, "Made from the best stuff on Earth," because that is what all the ads said. Since coming here I had tried portobello mushrooms, guacamole, and a cheese-filled pastry called *pupusa* that reminded me of a *paratha*, only it tasted even better. I had doodled Vikram's name across multiple pages, sketching hearts and flowers around it. I had written about the first time he had called me after I got here, how the softness of his voice made me ache for him. I had written about my mother, how distant and cold she had been, barely smiling, not really even speaking to any of us.

"But it will change!" I had written optimistically. "She knows we have no choice but to try and be happy with Papa's decision."

On this Sunday evening, the light was starting to fade outside. The weekend had been a welcome reprieve from the stress that was school. I sat alone in my room and looked through the pages of my diary. There was "homesickness" and "loneliness" on page two. Beneath that was "sadness," but I picked up a pen and put a neat line through it when I remembered that I had felt sad the day *chachi* Rekha, wife of *chacha* number two Pramod, had died. It had happened in such a haphazard, needless way: tripping over her sari and tumbling down a flight of steps.

In place of sadness, I now wrote the word *excluded*, something that had never been a part of my life before. In my old house I couldn't feel left out if I'd wanted to. During birthday celebrations and wedding anniversaries, everyone gathered in the big main hall to eat cake that Dadi would order from a local bakery. Even though I saw most of my family members every day, these parties were special.

Now, next to "excluded," I wrote a few more words that were hard for me to write. "No plans for Diwali." The new year, the biggest holiday in India, was around the corner, and nobody was even discussing it—no talk of festivities, fireworks, or gift giving. It was as if it didn't exist.

Later that evening I folded laundry with my mother and my father and helped Sangita with her homework.

"What shall we do for Diwali?" I asked, as if it were a thought that had just that second popped into my head. My mother looked at me coldly.

"What will we do? We will sit here alone, like we have done every night since your father brought us to this place." My mother's mood was off again, as it had been almost constantly since we got here.

My father stopped what he was doing.

"Please, Asha, don't worry. I have been thinking about it. We will celebrate as normal."

"How?" my mother demanded. "There is nobody to celebrate with."

My father's voice turned appeasing.

"We will do prayers at home, like we always do. The girls can buy new clothes. We will visit the temple in the evening. We will connect with people. We will find a community here."

I started to feel just a little more hopeful. There was something about anticipating Diwali that always put me in a celebratory mood. Even here, thousands of miles away from the extended family I'd always shared it with, the thought of it stirred some excitement in me.

I glanced toward my mother, hoping to see even a glimmer of the same anticipation. But instead, she gazed up from a fresh, dry peach towel she had clasped beneath her chin and looked right through me.

Sangita and I were excited to wake up on Diwali morning. There was an air of newness around us, a sense of possibilities. Our father had even suggested that we take the day off from school. I was tempted—any reason at all not to have to go in!—but Sangita said she didn't feel right about it, that if it wasn't technically a holiday, we must proceed as usual. I forced myself to agree with her.

We said our prayers at our makeshift temple and came running downstairs. "Diwali *mubarak!*" My father beamed, wishing Sangita and me a "Happy Diwali" with a slight hug and a big smile. He had already spoken to his parents, and Vikram would be calling me soon.

Our mother was in the kitchen, her back turned to us, stirring something on the stove.

"Ma, Diwali *mubarak!*" Sangita and I ran to her,

throwing our arms around her waist. She turned around. Her eyes were pink, her nose runny.

"Happy Diwali to you girls," she said tearfully, hugging us both. "May God bless and protect you."

"Ma, don't be sad," I said to her. "It is a beautiful day, and we will make the most of it. Please."

She wiped her eyes and blew her nose with her *dupatta*. She wished us a good day at school and turned back to her cooking.

At school, the pressure to have a good day felt even more heightened. My grandparents had taught me that how the year begins is how it will go on. As a result, it was crucial that I was, if not exactly thrilled and jubilant, at least not miserable. If I could just get through the day without being teased, humiliated, or poked fun at, then maybe there would be hope for me yet. And it seemed the goddess Laxmi, whose auspices are sought on the day, had listened to me after all: I was left alone. Nobody talked to or befriended me, but they didn't make fun of me either. It was a small mercy.

That night when it grew dark outside, my father turned on as many lights as he could, honoring the Diwali tradition of beckoning Laxmi, the goddess of prosperity, into homes. My mother walked around, turning them all off.

"No point wasting electricity," she said bitterly.

My father didn't argue with her.

"Asha, please get dressed," he said. "Let's go to the temple for prayers and celebrations. Mr. Jeremy has offered to take us."

I looked excitedly over at Sangita. I knew she was as keen to go as I was. We both wanted to wear Indian clothes and go to a place filled with other Indians. We looked at our mother pleadingly.

"You go. I'm not interested," she said, sitting down in front of the TV and picking up the remote. "Nothing is there for me. We don't even know anybody. We'll go and stand around like fools."

"Asha, you're not making sense," my father said, a note of irritation creeping into his voice. "How will we meet people unless we go out and try? We can introduce ourselves to the priest. We can tell him we are new here. He will help us find other families to befriend. But by staying home like this, Asha, nothing will happen; our lives will not improve."

"I'm going to sleep," my mother said, slapping the remote down on the table. "Go if you want."

She rose and went upstairs without turning back. Papa, Sangita, and I looked at one another. My sister's bottom lip was quivering. I put my arm around her.

"I'm sorry, girls, but we'll have to have a quiet Diwali

at home this year," my father said, trying to hide the disappointment in his eyes. "But see, all is not lost." He went to his briefcase and pulled out a package. "Mr. Jeremy gave me this today, in celebration." In my father's hand was a small pink cardboard box. We opened it and saw that it was filled with soft, spongy, sweet *ladoos*, a traditional Diwali dessert. "He got it at the Indian store. They are not like your grandmother makes at home, but it was a nice gesture."

The three of us sat down, pulled out some paper napkins from a small holder, and ate in silence.

Eight

AT SCHOOL A FEW DAYS LATER, large purple posters were being put up advertising the Halloween Rock Horror Show. The school gym would be transformed into a haunted house for a Gothic rock concert. There would be Crypt Cupcakes and I Scream Cones and Ghoulish Gateaux and Blood Punch. The whole school was invited.

Sangita and I stared up at one of the posters.

"What do you think?" she asked.

"I think it's silly," I said. "It has nothing to do with us."

"I think it looks like fun," my sister replied. "Amy mentioned it to me. She wants to go. Some of our friends are going."

Her words were like a stab to my heart, the way she

said "our friends," because she had them and I didn't. I didn't want to be comparing myself to my younger sister, but I was wondering why it had been so easy for her and so hard for me.

She saw the look on my face, and her smile disappeared.

"But you're right, *didi*," she said. "It is silly. Let's not go."

A note had been sent to all of the parents that students were allowed, even encouraged, to dress up for Halloween. My father first suggested that we go in our "best frocks," and I cringed at the thought. Then he told us to find one of the saris we had brought from India, remarking that we would stand out in a crowd in all that silk and gold finery. I didn't say as much to my father, but the last thing I wanted to do was accentuate the fact that I was Indian. I still attracted snickers sometimes when I spoke up in class, some of the students mocking my accent. Others went so far as to do a full-on imitation, wobbling their heads as they spoke as they imagined all Indians did. They told unfunny jokes about IT geeks and gas station owners. By now I had learned to ignore them. It still hurt, but I wasn't going to let them see that.

Still, arriving at school on Halloween morning was like stepping into a bizarre dream. There was Pippi

Longstocking, Spider-Man, a bunny rabbit, a shepherd. Cars spilled out Power Rangers, firemen, Wonder Woman, and girls in pink wigs. Even the teachers, who had, in my mind, always been the model of restraint and self-control, came in costume. People laughed as they greeted each other, complimented one another on their outfits. Sangita and I stood by in our regular pants and shirts, our satchels over our shoulders. Sangita looked at me a little sorrowfully. I patted her on the shoulder.

I made my way to class quickly and quietly, like I always did. I sat at the back, waiting for class to start and watching as my classmates, now transformed into a parade of wild characters, filed in one by one. There was a Betty Boop, a vampiress, a couple of M&M's, and three zombies. Sasha was carrying a tiny puppy in a bag and wearing a miniskirt and high heels. In my few weeks here, at least I now knew how to recognize Paris Hilton. Magali followed close behind.

I gasped when I saw her. She had pulled her hair into a single, thick braid that lay flat down her back. Using a black pencil, she had joined her eyebrows together and had drawn some short, slight whiskers along her upper lip. A fake set of braces gleamed through her parted lips. Her body was covered in a dress: a frilly white blouse attached to a knee-length pleated black skirt. I knew that dress. It was mine, my best one, the one I had worn on my first day of school. She had copied it exactly, down to the panty hose on her legs, her covered toes peeking through a pair of clunky black sandals. Her costume was me.

She caught my eye as she walked in and threw back her head in laughter. Some of my classmates laughed with her, while some of the others, seeing the look on my face, squirmed uncomfortably in their seats. Mr. White, now standing at the head of the class, said only a cursory "Settle down" before instructing his students to direct their attention to a particular chapter. But I couldn't really hear him; his voice was flattened out by the pressure that seemed to be building in my head, the spiky heat I was feeling all over my skin, the large lump that was sitting in my throat and prohibiting me from even swallowing, even breathing.

The rest of the day was sheer misery for me. A few of the students in my class whom I would run into in the hallways pointed at me and giggled behind their notebooks, while others averted their eyes, perhaps picking up on my embarrassment. I felt angry, angry that even after a few weeks here people still felt the need to pick on me, and angrier still that I didn't have a clue what to do about it.

At home that night I picked up my pink diary with the creeping vine on the front. I went back to the line that had "sadness" on it, the one I had crossed out, and wrote it back in again.

Nine

SIX WEEKS AFTER WE ARRIVED in America, my father bought a secondhand burgundy Toyota Camry.

"We will be free to go where we wish, like regular Americans!" he said. Even without the car he had wanted to be an active participant in this new American life, talking longingly of exploring faraway places: Yosemite and Sonoma, Ojai and Oxnard. He liked to experiment with different foods, to connect with people and forge friendships. Part of him wanted to be like the American man he had pictured in his head. I half expected to come home one day and find him holding a pair of tongs, standing next to a sizzling grill, a dog wagging its tail at his feet. He would happily open up a conversation with the person waiting in front of him in line at the bank, segueing into how he had just come from India, how it was his first trip abroad, and my, how lovely and clean were the roads here—no bullock carts! And so terribly efficient the services! And who knew so much was available in all those huge stores! He said people liked hearing how their country offered so much. He said it made them proud.

"Asha, we now have a car! We are mobile!" he said enthusiastically.

My mother grunted from the couch, from where she had been watching an Indian game show. My father had had a few Indian channels added to our satellite TV programming, figuring that it might help ease my mother's homesickness.

"I'm not interested in seeing any more of this place," she said.

I looked at my father, both of our faces registering dismay. Neither of us knew what to do for her. It seemed the more we tried to reach out, the further she pulled back. I had a nagging feeling that it was no longer just a case of extreme homesickness, that there was something far more serious going on. She was gradually falling apart, but nobody ever talked about it; it was as if we all hoped that by not drawing attention to it, it would go away. I was convinced that if we left it alone, my old mother would return: the happy, cheerful, busy one; the one who saw all the children of our household as her own, never failing to step in to tie a shoelace, blow a nose, plop a straw into a freshly opened coconut.

I missed her, and I wanted her back.

Two days later, Sangita and I got home from school, rang the doorbell, and were surprised that nobody answered. This had never happened before; my mother, for all her depression and sadness, had at least opened the door to us.

"Maybe she's in the bath, or sleeping," Sangita said to me. We waited a few more minutes. The garage door was open; the entrance to the house through it was unlocked.

"Ma!" I called out, walking up the stairs. "We are home!" We went into our parents' bedroom. She wasn't there, nor was her purse.

"Maybe she went for a walk," Sangita suggested. I could tell that even she didn't believe it. My mother never went anywhere alone, not even for a stroll down the street.

We went back downstairs. There was no food on the stove. We called Papa at work, who said he had no idea where my mother was.

We waited for ten more minutes, glancing out the window anxiously and looking everywhere for a note that she might have left. I called my father again, and within thirty minutes the Camry came gliding up the street.

My father rushed in, sat down, and put his face in his hands.

"Your mother has not been well," he said, looking up at us. "She has not been the same since we left home. I thought that after a few weeks here, a month even, she would adjust. But she is more miserable than ever. I am really worried."

My father stood up, put on his jacket, and went outside, Sangita and I trailing along behind him. He walked across the street and knocked on a door. A tall, bald man in a blue flannel shirt opened it.

"Excuse me, sir, I am so very sorry to be bothering you in the evening. My name is Girish Agarwal. We are new here. We live across the street. I was wondering if you might have seen my wife? She has been missing for some hours, and I do not know who else to ask. She would have been wearing some traditional clothing."

The man extended his hand. "George Roberts," he said. "Sorry, I wish I could help you. But I haven't seen her."

My father turned to go. The man spoke up again.

"I'm sorry it's taken us this long to meet," said the

man. "My wife and I have been meaning to come over with a casserole. We don't want you thinking that this is an unfriendly neighborhood," he said.

"Of course not," my father replied genially. "It is kind of you to have even thought of it."

"You know, let me quickly ask my wife," he said. "Betsy!" he yelled out. "Can you come here a second?"

Mr. George's wife came to the door. I had often seen her walking purposefully down the street, a weight in each hand, her short, curly, gray hair bouncing as she went. She was short and wide in the back and reminded me of Dadi.

"Well, hello there." She smiled. "Please, come in."

"You are most kind, but we are very anxious," said my father. "My wife has gone missing. It has been some hours. We were wondering if perhaps you might have seen something?"

"Oh, yes, I did see her," Betsy said, the eyes behind her green-framed spectacles brightening. "Must have been around one this afternoon. She was standing by the bus stop on Dover Drive."

My father frowned, his usually round and happy face suddenly stressed.

"Thank you, Mr. George, Mrs. Betsy," he said, extending his hand. "I'm certain that with your help I will be able to locate her. The next time we meet, it will be under more pleasant circumstances."

Following our father's lead, we walked quickly to the bus stop. My father squinted as he peered at the lists of stops for the three lines that ran through there. He looked away, scratched his head, and squinted again.

"Come, girls. Let's go home and get the car. I think I know where she is."

Ten

WE SAW HER, seated at the back at a small table surrounded by four black plastic chairs. Her hands were around a white Styrofoam cup; her head was bent above it. Ranjit Singh, the owner of Delhi Delites and Supplies, looked over the counter at us. We rushed up to my mother.

"Asha, what are you doing here?" my father asked, alarmed. "We have been so worried about you!"

My mother looked up, her eyes vacant. Under the bright fluorescent lights, she looked pale, the circles under her eyes darker than I had ever noticed.

"*Bhai sahib*, so good you have come," Mr. Ranjit said, his navy turban wobbling atop his head. "For hours she has been sitting here. Of course, that is okay, all are welcome, but she did not seem well. She has only been sitting and drinking tea."

"Thank you," my father said. "I will take care of everything."

My father wrapped his arm around my mother's hunched shoulders and escorted her out to the car.

She was silent all the way home, only vaguely shaking her head at my father's various entreaties to communicate. Finally, as we rounded the street that led back to our house, he simply gave up.

At home, he took her up to the bedroom, helped her get into bed, and came back downstairs. Sangita and I were already busy making dinner. He went into the den, put his feet on the coffee table, and rested his head on the back of the couch. He looked shaken.

I brought dinner to him there, everything stacked neatly on a red plastic tray, and Sangita trailed behind. Kishore Kumar was wailing in the background again.

"What have I done, girls?" he asked, looking at both of us. "What was I thinking bringing you all so far away from home? And how did I think that this would be okay, that suddenly she would be herself again?"

"It's okay, Papa, you're busy with your new job," Sangita said. "Please don't feel bad. It's not your fault."

"If not mine, then whose?" he asked. "It was my idea

to come here. Your mother had nothing to do with it. I have taken you all away from everything you know. She feels it the most. Her family, her connections—I have ripped her away from all that she knows."

He closed his eyes and shook his head, his face filled with sadness. It hurt me to see him this way. But it had hurt me as much to find my mother sitting alone and despairing in the local Indian grocery store, as if it was her only comfort in this new world.

Before Sangita and I went to bed that night, we gently opened the door to our parents' room to check on our mother. She was lying on her side, a bedside lamp on, her eyes open. But as soon as she saw us, she pretended to fall asleep.

The next morning our mother came downstairs. I moved over on the couch where I was sitting, indicating to her to join us. My mother stared vacantly at the television screen but did not sit down. Then she went into the kitchen, made tea, and took a cup upstairs. I ran after her. She didn't turn around. She went to her room and shut the door in my face.

I was stunned at my mother's coldness and couldn't even summon the initiative to go and get dressed. Instead, I went into the room with the shrine. I gazed at all the statues, at their beatific smiles. These deities were supposed to grant us our hearts' desires. They were supposed to make us stronger, happier. That's what I had been taught by my grandparents. That if we did good and prayed hard and showed appreciation for everything, our lives would unfold in a blessed way. Now, standing in front of the small marble figurines I had grown up with, the same ones I always bowed down to and chanted religious verses in front of, I wasn't feeling the way I was supposed to. I wasn't feeling grateful, or peaceful, or content. I wanted my mother to be herself again. This time, I didn't bow my head or say a prayer. There seemed to be no point.

That evening my parents argued in their bedroom.

"You need to see a doctor," my father said.

"Nonsense," my mother replied.

"Your behavior is not normal. We have been here more than a month. It's time to snap out of it." He paused. "I hate what you have become."

Silence.

I sat on my bed, clutching my diary to my chest, rocking back and forth, grateful that Sangita was at Amy's and didn't have to hear this. I hated the unhappiness that seemed to have fallen over my family, the discord between my parents. The contented couple with whom I had grown up, with the kind of unruffled marriage that was the model of what I would one day have with Vikram, had disappeared. I didn't even recognize the couple in the bedroom next door.

A few days later, my father said it was time to invite Mr. Jeremy over for dinner.

"He wants to meet the family," my father said. "I will tell your mother. She will have to make an effort, for one night at least."

We went shopping the night before the dinner, at one of the airport hangar–sized supermarkets that were all over this city. I was mesmerized by the offerings: bags of chips that were the length of my torso, containers of muffins and croissants that would feed a dozen hungry children in one sitting. Such a place would have been a dream for my family in Bangalore, given how many mouths had to be fed on a daily basis.

My father loaded up on sodas, juices, chips, and dip.

"Papa, that's a lot," I said, motioning to the rapidly filling shopping cart. "It's only Mr. Jeremy, right?"

"Yes, *beta*. But I want to offer him a choice of beverages and snacks. Also, it will not harm us to have these things in our house, for whenever people stop by," he said a little hopefully.

On our way home we stopped at Delhi Delites and

Supplies, where Mr. Singh inquired after our mother and showed us the fresh desserts we had come in for.

"What do you recommend? It is for a dinner party tomorrow," my father announced proudly.

The man slid open the case and pulled out several pieces of the diamond-shaped *kaju barfi*—the Indian dessert made with cashews—their smooth, cream-colored surfaces covered in delicate silver foil and sprinkled with chopped pistachios.

"Freshly made today, still good tomorrow," the man said, laughing heartily. "How many you want? Ten? Twenty?"

"A dozen will be fine," my father replied.

The next day I expected to find my mother in the kitchen, steeping and simmering and chopping. But she was not there. I went back upstairs and found her lying on her bed, still in her nightgown, re-reading an old Bollywood magazine.

"Ma, we are going downstairs to get everything ready for the arrival of Mr. Jeremy this evening," I said softly. "I thought we could prepare everything together?"

"You go," she said. "I'll come down soon."

My sister and I fetched pots and pans from the cupboards and laid out the jar of *ghee* and the small plastic containers of grated ginger, minced garlic, sliced onions, and chopped cilantro that were always at the ready in our refrigerator.

Sangita and I sat at the tall stools next to the kitchen counter and looked at each other. We both knew how to cook—all the girls of our household had been taught from an early age, literally at the feet of our grandmother, in preparation for the lives we would lead one day as wives and mothers. Even though we had servants, we were never allowed to assume that we would be waited on hand and foot, like the men of the house were. We were still children after all, and girls at that. In the hierarchy of the household, we ranked the lowest.

But still, we had never prepared a full meal from scratch on our own. We didn't know what to do next. We bided our time. Soon it was almost noon, and there was still no sign of our mother.

I looked over at Sangita. I could tell that she was thinking the same thing as me. Our mother wasn't coming downstairs. This was going to be the first time that she wasn't going to cook for a guest. There must be something really wrong with her.

"Heat some oil," I said to my sister.

Six hours later we were done. My mother would have been able to cook seven dishes in half the time. But

Sangita and I were new at this. At least we hadn't burned anything. By six thirty the kitchen was clean, and Sangita and I were in our best frocks. When the doorbell rang, we stood anxiously behind our father as he opened the door.

"Hello, Jeremy! Welcome! Welcome!" he said. "Please, come in. These are my girls, Shalini and Sangita."

Mr. Jeremy stepped in. He was shorter than I had imagined. He was wearing a smart checked shirt tucked into navy pants and in one hand was carrying a slender paper bag with a floral design. He shook my father's hand before turning to Sangita and me.

"Hey, great to meet you," he said. He extended his hand to my sister and then to me. I was immediately struck by his accent—so perfectly American with all those rolling *r*'s, to me so incongruous coming from an Indian.

"Please come in and have a seat," I said.

He moved into the living room, took a seat on the couch, and leaned into a cushion.

"Mr. Jeremy, what may I bring you to drink?" I asked. "We have Fanta, Coke, Sprite, apple juice, orange juice, club soda, of course water . . ." I rattled off, recalling the large bottles that we had stuffed into the refrigerator yesterday.

"Just call me Jeremy," he said. I nodded, knowing I wouldn't. "I'd love a beer."

My father looked over at us aghast. In all of his purchases yesterday, it had not occurred to him to buy beer.

"I'm sorry, but we don't have any," I said.

"It's no problem," my father shouted, jumping up. "I'll run down to 7-Eleven. It's just on the corner. Please, tell me which brand I should buy?"

"Relax," my father's boss said. "I can do without. A Coke would be fine. Anyway, I brought this," he said, handing me the bag in his hand. I looked inside; it contained a bottle of wine. "Maybe we can enjoy it together later, over dinner?"

"Actually, Jeremy, in my family we don't drink," my father said. Jeremy looked surprised. There was no reason he should have known that; this was the first time my father and his new boss were socializing. But it was true: my grandparents had a strict no-meat and no-alcohol rule, although I often wondered how my male cousins coped when they went with their friends to some of Bangalore's famous pubs.

"Please, let me open the bottle for you," my father offered, although I knew he didn't have a clue how to do so.

"No, thank you, it's fine," Jeremy replied. "Maybe

you can regift it," he added, smiling.

My father had put some music on the CD player to help liven up the otherwise quiet living room. On the table in front of Mr. Jeremy were the traditional Indian appetizers that Sangita and I had prepared. The *khandvi*, almost like pasta rolls but made of chickpea flour and yogurt, were floppier than they should have been, but Mr. Jeremy beamed happily when he tried one, saying he hadn't had any since visiting his grandparents in India a year earlier.

"I'm looking forward to meeting your wife," he said to my father, wiping some tamarind chutney off his fingers.

"Yes, she's just getting ready," my father said. "You know how women are!" He laughed weakly.

"Yeah, tell me about it," Mr. Jeremy said. "My ex-girlfriend used to take so long to get dressed I'd be tempted to leave without her. In fact, once I think I did!"

"So you are no longer with her?" my father asked. I was sitting on my hands, leaning forward, quite fascinated by this man.

"No, we split up about six months ago. It was too much work. It's true, you never really know anyone until you live with them; and after a few months of living with her, I realized I should get out before things got any worse."

Sangita and I turned and stared at each other. We had never before heard of an Indian man living with a woman who wasn't his wife.

"And she was American, this girl?" my father asked matter-of-factly.

"No, a *desi* just like me. My parents would have been thrilled if I'd gone through with it, gotten married and the whole thing; but I just couldn't do it."

I was even more shocked—an *Indian* woman living with an Indian man! What did her parents think? Did they even know? I had so many questions but bit my bottom lip instead of asking them. My parents had always taught me not to be too nosy about other people's affairs.

"Can I use the restroom?" Mr. Jeremy asked, standing up.

My father took the opportunity to run upstairs to see after our mother, Sangita and I tailing close behind.

"Asha, please, what are you doing?" my father beseeched. My mother was sitting on a small chair in front of the dressing table, gazing at herself in the mirror. She was still in her nightgown. "Please, you need to come down now. Our guest has been here almost one hour. It is very rude of you. He is my boss, Asha. You must at least make an appearance."

Our mother looked at the three of us and sighed

deeply, as if we were a source of huge irritation. Then she stood up, started unbuttoning her nightgown, and shut the door. My father went downstairs, while Sangita and I waited outside, like sentries to her sanity.

When she opened the door again, she looked like the mother we had always known. A trail of bright red *sindoor* was placed down the part in her hair. A smidgen of *kohl* lined her eyes, rouge on her cheeks. Next to her *mangalsutra* was a long gold chain with an enameled pendant with a picture of Lord Shiva. Her hair was combed straight. She was wearing a light yellow eyelet lace *salwar kameez* with matching bangles on her wrist and the same colored *bindi* in the middle of her forehead. I had forgotten how nice looking my mother was, how delicate her features, how large her eyes, which seemed to have been so cloudy recently. But there was still something frail about her.

My sister and I stood on either side of her as if to prop her up and to keep her from turning around and going back into the bedroom.

Downstairs, Mr. Jeremy stood as we walked in, his hand extended in greeting. My mother wanly took it.

"Asha, this is my boss, Jeremy," my father said, visibly relieved. "He's been very much enjoying the *dhokla* and *khandvi* the girls have prepared for him. But perhaps it is time to move to the dinner table?"

My mother didn't even sit down, instead going straight from the living room to the kitchen, Sangita and I following her. She opened the covered pots on the stove and lifted the aluminum foil we had placed over some of the serving dishes to keep their contents warm. She turned to Sangita and me, a look of surprise on her face.

"You girls did all this?" she asked. We both nodded. She looked sad again, almost sorrowful.

"I'm sorry I didn't come downstairs to help you," she said.

At the dining table, Mr. Jeremy sat back in his chair, his mouth open, his eyes wide.

"What a spread!" he exclaimed. "You made all this at home, and for one guest?"

"It is not the number of guests, but how much we honor them," my father said in response.

Mr. Jeremy cast his eyes over the offerings: a carrot-and-coriander soup that steamed in its glass tureen, a creamy white yogurt *raita* reddened with fresh beetroot, a big platter of tamarind rice, and spinach folded into fried bread. We had fried large green chilies and served them soaked in gravy and Indian cottage cheese and peas simmered in vegetables and spices. We had hoped that all our efforts would make him feel welcome. It might have been because of him that our lives had been uprooted, but I remembered the pride in my father's eyes the day he had come home in Bangalore and told us he had been offered this job. Just for making my father happy, I wanted to thank Mr. Jeremy.

My father, seated next to his boss, leaned over and served him first. Mr. Jeremy protested and said he would help himself. Then my mother served my father, as she always did whenever we ate together, while Sangita and I waited our turns to eat.

"This is incredible!" Mr. Jeremy said, tucking into his food. "I can't remember the last time I tasted Indian food this good." He laughed and raised his glass. He seemed so much more relaxed now compared to when he first got here, when it looked as if he couldn't wait to get away. "Where did you girls learn to cook like this?"

"Our *dadi*," Sangita said. "Also, all our *chachis*. And of course, our mother. At home, in India, we used to help in the kitchen every day."

Mr. Jeremy nodded thoughtfully and then turned his attention to my mother.

"So tell me, Asha, how have you been enjoying your time here so far? I know it takes awhile to settle in."

My father looked anxiously over at my mother, his shoulders hunched.

"Everything is okay," she said, averting her eyes.

My father's shoulders relaxed again.

"You know, LA is a great city to live in," Mr. Jeremy said. "There's just so much going on. I moved here from Philly, and I really love it. The weather, the beaches, the people are so easygoing and friendly."

My mother flinched. She bit her bottom lip. The food on her plate sat untouched. She coughed a small cough and played with the corner of her napkin.

"I mean, don't get me wrong," Mr. Jeremy continued. "India is great. My grandparents are there, lots of relatives. It's totally booming, *especially* cities like Bangalore, Delhi, Mumbai. Compared to what it was ten years ago, it's crazy how much progress there is. But I have to tell you, I wouldn't give up life in America for anything. India can be kind of aggravating, trying to get anything done. It's still a Third World country. You guys are lucky you're here." He paused for a minute to place an overflowing spoon full of rice into his mouth.

I turned to look at my mother. Her nostrils were flared, her jaw clenched.

"You think you have done us a favor, do you?" she said bitterly. She barely opened her mouth to let the words through. Her eyes were fixed on our guest.

"What?" he asked, puzzled.

"You think you have done us a great favor by bringing us here, as if we were beggars in need of rescuing? Is that what you are saying?" my mother asked again.

"Asha, please, I don't think Mr. Jeremy meant any such thing," my father pleaded, his face turning red. "He was simply making conversation."

"You do not have the right to come here and sit at my table and eat my food and tell me that my life is better here than it was in India," my mother continued, scolding him now. "It is not. It never will be."

A heavy silence now fell over the table.

"Asha, please," my father said hesitantly. "Mr. Jeremy is our guest."

"Yes, he is," my mother continued, her face still stony. "And he is your boss. And I am here because I had no choice. But don't expect me to like it. I will do my duty as your wife; and when our time is up in this country, we will go back."

At that my mother neatly folded her napkin, stood up, adjusted her *dupatta* across her shoulders.

"Asha, I'm really sorry if I offended you," Mr. Jeremy said. He had put down his spoon and fork, and looked up at my mother apologetically. "I didn't intend to hurt your feelings. If I can help in some way, please tell me."

His sincerity touched me, and I hoped it would soften

my mother's stance. But she didn't sit down.

"I'm not feeling well," she said. "Good night." She went back upstairs, and we heard her shut the door firmly behind her.

I felt my stomach drop out of my body, as if there was nothing holding me together. All these weeks, my mother hovered at the periphery of our lives. She was there sometimes—in the kitchen, or in front of the TV— perhaps taciturn and unsmiling, but at least a shadow of her was present. And she would never, ever be rude to a guest, or walk out in the middle of a dinner gathering.

Now, tonight, after this outburst, I knew that a big part of my mother's identity was gone. I wondered how I'd ever be able to reach her again.

A few days later as I was scrubbing the pressure cooker after dinner, the phone rang. I raced to it, hoping it might be Vikram.

"Hey! Is that Shalini or Sangita?"

It was Mr. Jeremy.

"It's me, Shalini," I said. "I'll go get my dad for you."

"No, wait!" he said quickly. "I was actually calling for you."

Eleven

THE FOLLOWING SATURDAY MORNING, my father, Sangita, and I loaded up the car with Pyrex dishes full of food, a thick blanket, a soccer ball, and some fold-up chairs. Half an hour later, we pulled into a large, grassy park with playground equipment at the far end, a basketball hoop off to one side, picnic tables, and barbecue pits in the center. Mr. Jeremy was laying out plastic plates and cups. He looked over at us and waved. Next to him was an Indian couple about my parents' age and an Indian girl who was about mine. She was wearing a white sweater, black jeans, and boots. Her hair was cut to about her chin. Even from a distance I could see she was pretty. I approached with my sister and my father, and she waved as if she had known us forever.

"Great, you made it!" said Mr. Jeremy, shaking all of our hands.

He made the introductions. Haresh Idnani; his wife, Poonam; and their daughter, Renuka. Old friends from Philadelphia, living now in LA.

"Hello, uncle, aunty," I said, addressing the elders first as I had been taught to do. "It's very nice to meet you." Simply being able to call someone "uncle" and "aunty," with all the familiarity that that conveyed, was a treat.

Aunty Poonam asked where my mother was. My father replied that she was "not feeling herself" and left it at that.

Renuka reached out to greet me with a hug. Tiny crystal earrings dangled from her lobes.

We helped ourselves to food; we had prepared traditional Indian snacks while Renuka's family brought green salad, garlic bread, pasta, a box of tangerines.

"Run off, girls; get to know each other!" cooed Aunty Poonam, smiling widely, the way my mother used to smile. Uncle Haresh started telling my father about his aerospace engineering job. Renuka feigned a yawn, and I giggled. We took our plates and settled down on the blanket.

"You just got here from India, right?" asked Renuka, folding a piece of lettuce into her mouth and looking at my sister and me as if we were curios in an antique store.

"Yes, from Bangalore."

"Wow, that's epic," she said. "I can't even imagine what it must be like, coming from there to here."

With very little prompting from Renuka, Sangita chatted enthusiastically about how much she liked school and her new friends, how easy the homework was. She talked like a kid who had just returned from Disneyland. I envied her happiness.

"What about you?" Renuka asked, turning to me when Sangita went off to get some juice. "How do you like it?"

"It's not a bad place," I said, my tone markedly flatter than my sister's. I turned around to make sure Sangita wasn't within earshot. "But I am finding it hard to fit in. The other kids at school are not so nice to me; and, unlike my sister, I haven't made any friends there yet."

It was a relief to say it aloud. With my father and Sangita, I always had to pretend. Vikram had some idea of how unhappy I was, but not the full extent of it. Here was a girl I had only known for an hour, but I felt like telling her everything.

Renuka put her plate down on the blanket and wiped some crumbs off her fingers. The sun had dipped down behind a mountain, cooling the air. I wanted to go to the car and get a jacket but didn't want to tear myself away from the conversation.

"I've never been to India," Renuka said. I tried not to show my shock. I couldn't fathom the possibility of an Indian person who had never been to India.

"My dad came here as a kid; he married my mom here; I was born in this country. We have some relatives in Mumbai, but nobody I really know. All my grandparents are here. I've never had a reason to visit India, which is stupid, I know, because I shouldn't need a reason.

"So because I've never been there, and I don't know what your life was like, I can't really give a lot of advice. High school can be really fun. But you know nothing's gonna just fall into your lap, right? If you want to be happy here, you need to kinda make it happen. If you want friends, you need to go make them. You gotta make an effort. Seriously."

Those words lingered in my head for the rest of the afternoon, as we three girls threw a ball to one another, swung on the swings like preschoolers, and chatted about the latest movies and our favorite TV shows over steaming hot tea from a thermos. It was the single happiest day I'd had since arriving in America.

Later as we rode home, my father asked Sangita and me if we had enjoyed meeting our new friends.

I nodded as I gazed out of the front passenger side window.

"Renuka is really, really nice," I said.

"Yes, she seems to be a very good girl," my father agreed, turning on his indicator light to merge into another lane. "Very straightforward, honest, and polite. I talked to her while we were having *chai* after lunch. And I said to her, 'You are how my Shalini would be if she was brought up in America.' Was I wrong to say that, *beta*?"

"No, Papa," I said quietly. "I think you're quite right."

Renuka called me the next morning, uttering the three words that I had longed to hear from someone ever since I had gotten here.

"Wanna hang out?" she asked, smacking noisily on a piece of gum.

My heart actually jumped in my chest. In a flash I had visions of Renuka and me being like the other girls I had seen in school, the ones who went home with their friends after class, texted each other constantly, and talked excitedly about going to the movies or bowling or shopping. The fun of a girlhood friendship was something I had missed. I wanted to be like Sangita, who had lately taken to going off after school with Amy in her mother's SUV. Amy had a heated pool in her backyard, and Sangita loved spending time there. She often stayed over for dinner. Many times, she asked me to go along with her. But being asked by my kid sister to join in with her and her friends because I didn't have any friends of my own made me almost want to cry.

Now, here was a girl calling just for me.

"Yes, I'm free today," I said happily. "What shall we do?"

After Renuka and I made our plans, I rushed upstairs to get dressed. I stopped in at the prayer room. I hadn't been in there in a few days, which was unusual for me. I had begun to lose faith. My mother was miserable; I had been miserable. But now, on this beautiful Sunday, I began to feel just a little more hopeful. I bowed my head in thanks. Then I gently knocked on the door to my parents' bedroom. My mother was in a chair, looking out the window. She was still in her nightgown, a Kleenex folded in one hand.

"I'm going out, Ma," I said. I wanted her to share my enthusiasm, to be happy for me, to tell me to have a good time. Instead, she looked right through me, nodded, and went back to looking at the scenery outside the window.

My father dropped me off at a mall halfway between our house and Renuka's. She was standing next to a fountain inside, a small, sparkly handbag slung over her shoulder. Even though she looked trendy, I wasn't intimidated by it. And unlike the other girls in my school, she didn't look me up and down when I walked in.

"Sorry I'm late," I said.

"No problem. I got here early. I always worry about not being able to find a parking spot."

"You drove?" I asked, shocked. She and I were the same age, and I couldn't imagine myself behind the wheel of a car. In India, the family shared a number of cars and drivers. None of the women of the house had ever had to transport themselves anywhere.

"Yup," she said proudly. "Got my learner's permit the day I turned fifteen and a half. My mom was in the car with me. That's by law." She rolled her eyes. "She had to do some errands around here anyway. But I'm getting hooked on the feeling of being able to get myself anywhere."

"Of course," I said, feeling even more like a child.

We went to the food court and had a chocolate milk shake and split a veggie burger and fries.

"It's so cool you could come out today," she said. "I liked talking to you yesterday."

"Me too," I said. "It was the longest conversation I've had with another girl since I got here. Except my sister, I mean."

"I hate that you're, like, not having a good time," she said. "You shouldn't be hanging out by yourself. There's so much for you to get involved in."

"I know," I said, thinking of the endless activities that happened at school: sports, music, the school paper, drama club, debate team. I hadn't been a part of any of it. My lack of interest aside, it was impossible. Schoolwork and looking after the house in the face of my mother's condition was more than enough to consume my time; I didn't need to add an extracurricular activity to the mix.

"I don't have time for anything new right now," I said. I wanted to tell Renuka about my mother, but she was still a new friend. I wasn't sure how much my father would want me to say.

"See, Shalini, this is what I mean," she said, a look of disappointment crossing her face. "Nothing happens on its own, especially in high school."

I sucked on my straw. The fact was, I didn't even know how to make friends. In Bangalore I was surrounded by kids my own age. There was always someone around to talk to, to play with, to hang out with. I'd never had to actually go out and befriend someone. I didn't even know where to start.

"The people at school don't seem very accepting

of me," I said. "I look as if I don't belong. Back home, nobody ever teased me."

Now Renuka let out a tiny grunt of frustration.

"This is America!" she said, waving one hand in the air. "It's all about diversity! The only thing that's stopping you from having a great social life is you. You just need to get out of your own way. Look at your sister. She has the right attitude. She jumped in. You have to do the same."

Tables around us were filled with chattering families. I couldn't hear myself think. I hated that Renuka was right. I hated that my baby sister had instinctively known what to do but I hadn't had a clue. And I hated that perhaps a part of me had *wanted* it like this, so that maybe I could wrap myself in my loneliness like an old and comfortable blanket. Perhaps the only way I was different from my mother was that she was more honest about her depression. I was simply the way I had always been in every aspect of my life: passive and unadventurous.

I looked up at Renuka and nodded weakly. Her face brightened.

"Listen, if it will make you feel better about yourself, do you wanna maybe get a makeover?"

I looked down at what I was wearing: black

elastic-waist pants that had been handed down to me by one of my cousins, and a T-shirt that had a picture of Tweety Bird on the front.

"Nothing major," she said. "Just a little hair trim, maybe a couple of new tees? You might feel more confident."

"Let's just walk around," I said. "My father only gave me twenty dollars. And I never buy anything unless my parents are with me."

We strolled past the shops, weaving our way in and out of the crowds. Renuka stopped outside a clothing store and grabbed me by the arm.

"Look," she said, gesturing to the window. "Awesome." The mannequins had on the type of clothes the girls at my school wore: strappy little dresses with high waists, jeans that were so tight they looked as if they had to be peeled off, T-shirts with funny sayings and cute pictures. Renuka pointed to leggings and a striped top.

"You could totally rock that with a great pair of boots," she said. "What do you think?"

I stood silently, still sucking on my straw, enjoying the hissing sound it made as it hit the ice at the bottom of the cup. I didn't want leggings, and I didn't want to rock anything. I didn't want anyone to make me over. I just wanted a friend.

"I'll think about it," I answered quietly. We continued walking in silence, half glancing in the shop windows. Something had come between us, something small and uncomfortable, like a splinter in a finger.

Renuka suddenly stopped walking.

"You know what?" she said. "I'm sorry. Forget what I said earlier. You don't need a makeover. You're totally fine as you are. You don't need to go around looking like all the other girls in school. People are gonna love you as you are, or they're not. You're you. Own it."

I tossed my cup into a nearby trash can and smiled.

I went home empty-handed, with the exception of a hair clip I'd picked out of a bargain bin in a clothing store, and only after Renuka told me that she liked it too.

When my father came to pick me up, all the way home in the car I couldn't stop thinking about all the things Renuka had said—not about buying new clothes (or not buying them) but about not being afraid anymore to just be myself, to find ways to be involved in school, to get out of my own way. I understood what she was trying to tell me. I just didn't know how to get there.

Twelve

I WAS YEARNING TO TALK TO VIKRAM that night. After my fun afternoon out, the quiet of the house was oppressive.

I hadn't told Renuka about him. At the mall she had occasionally pointed to a boy here and there, telling me how hot she thought he was. I had nodded agreeably. At one point I was about to say something, to hold up my ruby ring like the accomplishment it was. But I held back, fearing what she would think of me. A sixteen-year-old girl engaged from the age of three. She might have thought it pathetic.

Now, at home, I was profoundly lonely. I craved the clatter and chaos of my old home, Vikram—his beaming face when he came to visit, touching the feet of my grandparents in greeting and then taking me out, with a couple of cousins as chaperones, for a *chikoo* shake and to see the latest Bollywood film. We would sit in those dark, crowded theaters, our knees pressed against each other. I would turn and stare at his profile, silhouetted against the shadow-filled room: his slightly arched forehead, strong nose, high cheekbone, angular jaw. He was the handsomest boy around—handsomer even than the dashing heroes up on the screen. And he was mine.

I speed-dialed his number.

"Do you miss me?" I asked, almost as soon as he answered. I had never asked him that before. I just assumed that he would. But two months into our time here, with another twenty-two months stretching out endlessly before us, I wanted to hear it from him.

"Of course, Shalu," he said. "A lot. I go visit your *dada*, and it feels so strange not seeing you running down the stairs toward me. College is keeping me busy. But really, it's hard for me."

I suddenly felt unsettled. Vikram was a gorgeous, outgoing nineteen-year-old boy; and I wondered if perhaps he wasn't going to become like the other boys, interested in girls and parties. He was fun loving, self-assured. I was self-conscious about my braces, about my hair in that old-fashioned braid. Even compared to the families of other girls in India, my family was ultratraditional. My best friend's brother had recently gotten engaged to a French girl. One of my older cousin's schoolmates would be going off to a university in London. I knew that the college-going daughters of my parents' friends wore sleeveless tops and skirts and traveled in taxis on their own, met boys at the pubs. My grandfather would never permit any of that. He remained rooted in an old India, one that no longer existed outside of his longing for it.

Now, with me no longer in the way, maybe Vikram would welcome a chance to see who else was out there.

I couldn't bear to think about it.

"What's the matter?" he asked, sensing my discomfort.

"I'm feeling insecure. What if you meet someone else?" I couldn't believe the words were coming from my mouth, and I shook my head a little. Perhaps I had been watching too much American television.

He laughed.

"Never, Shalu," he said. "I came to see you on the day you were born. My mother tells me that our fates were sealed there and then."

"Yes," I said. "I know. But if your mother hadn't said that . . . if our fathers hadn't made the arrangements . . . would you, well, would you still feel that way? Would you still want me?" It was out there now. A question that had never been asked. Despite the strictures of our combined family units, would Vikram and I still have been drawn to each other?

"Even if our fathers were not best friends," he said quietly, "I would have loved you from the moment I saw you. Whether you were a baby or a grown woman. I would have seen the goodness in your heart, the sweetness of your nature; and I would have loved you."

I sighed with relief. God, I loved this boy.

After we hung up I lingered in the armchair, staring at the ring on my finger, remembering the day we had exchanged them.

Until that day there had been no official recognition of my engagement to Vikram. Thirteen years ago, my father had dutifully told his parents of the agreement, and Dada had matter-of-factly informed the rest of the household. The news had been received with little fanfare and even less surprise. The next morning, Dada had checked with our family astrologer. As I played in a makeshift sandbox, the astrologer had told Dada, "It's a good match; they will be happy, have children, live long lives." It had been all that Dada needed to hear.

I myself hadn't found out about it until I was eleven, when my grandmother told me as we cleaned rice in the kitchen, and only after I had told her that my all-girls convent school was soon going to have classes with boys. My grandmother had stiffened when she heard that, as if suddenly aware that I would soon have proximity to boys outside of my family, outside of Vikram.

"Keep to your girl friends," Dadi had instructed me. "For when you are of age, you and Vikram will be married. It is already arranged." And with that she removed a large black stone from the mound of rice and flung it behind her shoulder. I remember scraping off the grains of rice that stuck to my palms and racing out to the courtyard to find Sangita. She had been sitting in a rubber tire swing that swayed from an old oak tree. I grabbed her little hands and told her that one day Vikram would become her *jijaji*, her brother-in-law. She smiled at me, her mouth all gummy holes and half teeth, and went back to swinging. I had been elated, not just because I was going to marry Vikram, but because I was going to marry at all. It had been my only girlhood dream.

Thanksgiving was upon us before we knew it. For weeks now it had been everywhere. TV commercials showed supermarkets offering sale prices on turkeys, lavish spreads of mashed potatoes and green beans and corn bread, women with shiny lipstick and golden hair beaming at their guests. At school everyone had discussed their Thanksgiving plans: relatives flying in, a trip away. More than ever before, I felt the need to belong, to be invited to participate.

My father, not wanting his first Thanksgiving to pass him by, called Uncle Haresh to broach the idea of doing something together. Mr. Jeremy had already gone to Philadelphia to see his family. I sat next to my father on the couch, playing with the fringed edge of a velvet cushion.

"No, no, of course not, that's absolutely fine," my father said, looking a little disappointed. "Of course you've made other plans. But please don't worry about us; we will be fine, maybe do something quiet as a family."

He put down the phone and looked over at me. All these weeks, he had put on a brave face about everything. But now there was a holiday that was all about family and celebration, two things my father adored more than anything else in the world, and I could see he felt alone. We both did.

"It doesn't matter," he said. "It is not our holiday anyway."

On Thanksgiving Day, the street was more quiet than usual. Even the mothers and nannies who would stroll their babies outside weren't there today; the regular walkers and joggers stayed indoors. My mother hadn't emerged from her room for two days.

Sangita and I were sitting on the couch, our novels and knitting projects and schoolwork spread out on the coffee table before us. I would have given anything to be somewhere else at that moment, to be part of a group, laughing and eating, gathering around the TV afterward to watch a football game I didn't understand. But it was just us, with only one another to keep us company.

We gazed through the curtain of the living-room window and saw a car pull up outside the home of Mr. George and Mrs. Betsy. Two couples emerged, holding a bouquet of flowers, bottles of wine, a casserole dish. One of them rang the doorbell. Mr. George, wearing a big smile and a red sweater, answered it. Everyone hugged and shook hands. Behind him I saw several other people gathered in the foyer, drinking from long-stemmed glasses and laughing. It was just as I had seen in those TV commercials, all joy and merriment. Mr. George shut the door. I let the curtain fall. A brass clock on the mantelpiece ticked loudly. It was so quiet I could hear Sangita breathing. My sister and I looked at each other again, and I saw in her face the loneliness I had been hiding in mine.

Thirteen

DR. GUPTA WAS A LARGE WOMAN with a loud voice and a wide mouth rimmed by bright pink lipstick who wore her hair in a bun covered by a small black hairnet. The first opening she had was on the Thursday after Thanksgiving, and my father grabbed it. She was the only Indian female psychologist in a thirty-mile radius.

The weather had cooled, the days were shorter, and my mother was worse. It was a miracle she had left the house to go there, but my father had begged and then threatened. She barely even left her room anymore, especially since my father had put a TV in there, which she kept tuned permanently to Indian channels. Now, every time I passed her door I heard Indian news shows about landslides and labor unions, ads for jewelry stores and cooking oil. In that upstairs bedroom, with its beige curtains and picture of an oak-shaded country lake on a wall, my mother had shut out her new world and disappeared into the India she had left behind.

I was alone in Dr. Gupta's waiting room, mindlessly flicking through a copy of *Good Housekeeping*; my parents were in an examining room. Twenty minutes later my mother emerged, her eyes puffy, her nose red. Dr. Gupta had asked to speak to my father privately. My mother sat down in the chair next to mine. I put my hand on her arm, asked her how she was feeling, if she wanted a cup of water. She folded her arms in front of her, laid her head against the wall behind her, and closed her eyes.

On the way home we stopped at a nearby pharmacy to fill the prescription that the doctor had written. My father returned carrying a small bag containing a couple of orange bottles of pills, their labels a jumble of unpronounceable names and dosages. At home, my mother went upstairs to nap.

"Clinical depression," my father intoned, his face more serious than I was used to seeing it. "Dr. Gupta wants to run some tests to check for hormonal imbalances that might be compounding the problem." He sounded as if he was talking about an acquaintance rather than his own wife. "But for now we can only rely on two things: medicine and time."

"I like your hair like that," Renuka said as soon as I stepped out of my father's car. "The clip looks really nice."

I raised my hand to the shiny silver clasp, adorned with a small crescent moon and a crystal-studded five-point star, that held up my hair on one side. It was the one I had bought at the mall the first time I had gone out with Renuka. My hair was brushed straight and left loose instead of woven into the thick braid I had worn down my back for as long as I could remember, the one that had caused the vegetable vendors to refer to me as "*choti walli,*" the girl with the braid. Every morning since I was a little girl, my mother used to rub coconut oil in my hair and then braid it into a single plait. It was our moment of togetherness in a crowded household. We hadn't had many of those moments since my mother had gotten sick.

"Thanks," I said now to Renuka, smoothing my hair down in the back. "It feels different, but I like it too."

Our families had been seeing a lot of each other. The Idnanis had taken us to Santa Monica to ride the Ferris wheel and, one weekend, to Universal Studios.

One Sunday we had driven to Santa Barbara. On

the way home, Uncle Haresh suggested stopping at the boardwalk to get a whiff of the salty air and to feel the cool sand under our toes.

"It is like Chowpatty beach in Mumbai," my father had said wistfully. "We went there when you two girls were small. You were rescuing the fish that had washed ashore, throwing them back into the water." He'd smiled at the memory. "I will wait till your mother is well and then I will bring her here."

Now Renuka and I had gotten together to see a Hindi film at a little cinema in the Valley. She only agreed to go because there were English subtitles. Afterward we walked across the street to a South Indian restaurant known for its *dosas*.

"Hey, look," she said, pointing to a small pink flyer on the corkboard at the front of the restaurant. It said: PREMA'S TRADITIONAL INDIAN BEAUTY SERVICES. Renuka glanced over at me and then looked quickly at her watch.

"Come with me," she said, grabbing me by the wrist. "There's something I want you to have. My treat."

Prema, stout and middle-aged, reminded me of the lady who would come to our house in Bangalore at the behest of the women of the household to provide waxing, threading, and facials.

"I've had a cancellation," she said. "What do you

need?" She was looking directly at me, appearing to take in every pore on my face, every tiny wisp of hair covering its surface. She narrowed her eyes.

"Never been threaded?" she asked, staring right at my eyebrows, which had long ago started to join in the center. I shook my head. "Not even your upper lip?" she continued, this time turning her attention to the area directly above my mouth, which was covered in a layer of fine hair.

"My *dada* didn't want me to," I said. "He thought I was too young."

"You're straight from India?" she asked, ushering me into a room in the back that had posters of big-haired women in shiny evening gowns on the walls.

"Yes, I've just come here a few months back."

"Hah, but you are a girl in America now," she said, pushing me gently into a chair and pulling out a spool of white thread from her pocket. "Here, everything happens earlier."

Prema ended up working over my entire face, her thread slicing hair from my cheeks, chin, and sideburns as she blew away the soft, dark fuzz. It was terribly painful, and I wondered how my cousins and aunts could put up with it on a regular basis. Later, as she dabbed a tonic on my face, she took the liberty of hiking up my jeans from the ankles and peering at my legs. She *tut-tut*ted loudly.

"*So* hairy!" she announced loudly. "Just like a boy! Give me fifteen minutes; I do quick-quick waxing," she said, getting up to go fetch her supplies. I sat upright in the chair.

"No, please, this is enough for one day," I said. "I'll come back."

When I walked through the door at home, I smiled. My father had bought a small silver Christmas tree, which he had placed in the corner of our den and from which he had hung tiny, shiny, red and green glass balls. Underneath it was a cluster of prettily wrapped gifts. Fake snow had been sprayed around a glass window. There were two felt stockings hanging above the fireplace we had never gotten around to lighting; and a wreath had been placed in the middle of our dining table, a thick red pillar candle surrounded by plastic berries at its center. Sangita was arranging tinsel across the banister, her eyes shining.

I turned toward my father, a look of pleasant surprise on my face.

"When in America," he said, grinning, "do as the Americans!"

As Christmas break came to an end, my father took Sangita and me out to the postholiday sales. At Target,

Sangita and I selected glittery pens and notebooks with pretty pictures on the front and new tote bags. On the way to the cash register we stopped at the juniors clothing section and looked at fitted T-shirts with beading, corduroy jackets with patch pockets, frilly skirts that were worn over leggings. They were the things that the girls in my school wore. My father came over to us and asked if there was anything we liked, anything we wanted. Up until then our school wardrobe had consisted of loose cotton tunics from India worn over jeans, a sweatshirt on top.

"It's okay," my father said. "Try on a few things. You girls deserve it."

I glanced at Sangita nervously. I didn't know where to start. She rifled through the racks, pulled out a black cardigan with a sequin design on its pocket, a sweater that belted at the waist, a violet-colored blouse with a ruffle.

"Here," she said confidently, handing the hangers over to me. "These will look good on you."

Exhilarated, I went to the fitting room, shrugged into the cozy tops, and loved how I felt: stylish, but not so I'd never recognize myself. I decided that that was just where I wanted to be.

Right after, our father took Sangita and me to Renuka's

house for dinner. Aunty Poonam ordered in pizza and mozzarella cheese sticks. The TV was turned to HBO, but nobody was watching. After we ate, Sangita and I went up to Renuka's bedroom. The walls were covered with photos of Renuka and her friends at her school, postcards of places she had visited with her parents, and a large poster of Taylor Lautner. The three of us plopped down on her bed, which was shaped like a big, white, wooden sleigh, and started leafing through pages of a celebrity magazine while Renuka regaled us with gossip about people we had never heard of before.

"How cute is he?" She was pointing to a picture of Zac Efron.

"He has nice eyes," Sangita said, kneeling on the bed.

"He looks *just* like a guy at school I had the biggest crush on." Renuka giggled. "I was, like, totally crazy about him. But he hooked up with some other girl. What about you?" she asked me, lying on one side and resting her head in her hand. "Any guy at school you're crushing on yet? It's gonna happen sooner or later, you know."

"Come on, Renuka. You know *didi* is getting married, right?"

Renuka bolted up so quickly the magazines fell off her bed.

"Whoa!" she said. "What the hell?"

"Sorry, Renuka, that I didn't tell you. I didn't know what you would think," I said.

"I'm like your one and only BFF here," she teased. "I can't believe you've been holding out on me. I knew you lived with thirty-seven people, friggin' chaotic. But a guy you're going to marry? How could you not have told me?"

"His name is Vikram," I said. "His father and my father have been best friends for thirty years. He's nineteen now. On my third birthday, my father and his decided that when Vikram and I come of age, we should be married. We've been engaged ever since."

Renuka's eyes were wide, her mouth partly open, as if she was watching a horror film.

"A few weeks before coming to America, we exchanged rings." I showed her the ruby ring I wore. "He has exactly the same one. We talk and email as much as we can. I really miss him," I said quietly. I looked down at the floor, pushing my bare feet into Renuka's carpet. Sangita left us to get some more pizza. Renuka got up and closed the door.

"So, have you like, done it?" she asked me. The mischievous, vaguely conspiratorial look on her face told me what she meant.

"No!" I said vehemently.

"Seriously? Engaged for thirteen years and he hasn't

made a move? You've at least made out, right?" she asked.

I grew uncomfortable. This was not a conversation I had ever had with anyone.

"We're never alone together," I said. "We will wait until we are married to do anything."

"Oh my God!" she said finally, blinking. "So, listen, how do you know you love him? How do you know he's really the guy for you? I mean, like, what happens if he's a bad kisser?"

"It's really not the most important thing," I said. Funny how I'd never even given that a second thought, and here it was the first thing that came into Renuka's head.

"He's a good guy," I continued. "And I'm sure he's a great kisser." I was blushing now. "But even if he isn't, he's the boy I'm going to marry. He's kind and thoughtful and really loves me. That's more important than anything."

"Well, all I can say is, Wow," Renuka said. Her curiosity was satisfied, but I couldn't help thinking that she looked at me a little differently.

"Hey, no, I think it's great," she said, seeing the crestfallen look on my face. "I'll be stressing over college applications, and you'll be planning your wedding and finally losing your virginity. Wow."

fourteen

"SO YOU FINALLY USED OUR GIFT, did you?" Sasha snickered in homeroom. It took me a few seconds to realize that she was talking about the hair-removing cream she and Magali had given me.

I stiffened at first, the way I always did when either of those girls looked at me. But now I remembered Renuka telling me to stop being afraid, to develop some confidence. I stared up at Sasha from my desk, glancing at a peace pendant around her neck. How ironic: a peace emblem on a girl who delighted in tormenting me.

"Actually, I did use the gift," I said. "It came in very handy. So thank you. I hope I can return the favor sometime?"

Sasha was speechless, her eyebrows raised in surprise.

I picked up my bag and made my way to the next class, trembling as I walked.

For the rest of the day I felt strangely energized. There were moments when I thought about what I'd said to Sasha, remembered the look of astonishment on her face, and giggled about it, and held my head a little higher than usual.

At home later I phoned Vikram. I didn't tell him the exact circumstances of the exchange—I was too embarrassed to let him know that someone had teased me for having a lady-mustache and unibrow. But I told him that I hadn't run away and hid from one of the mean girls.

"I stood up to her," I said. "It won't be as much fun for her to pick on me anymore."

"I knew it, Shalu!" my lovely fiancé said. "Things will turn around for you now. You'll see."

Two weeks later, when we were getting our homework back in algebra class, I heard Charlie cursing under his breath at his grade. Mr. Jeffries handed me back my paper, which had a large, red, circled A on the top, the words *Well done!* scrawled underneath. I looked up again at Charlie, whose face was pale, clicking his pen nervously.

As we were leaving class, the teacher asked Charlie

and me to stay behind. I was puzzled. I couldn't have been in trouble. The classroom was now empty apart from the three of us. Mr. Jeffries adjusted his glasses.

"I want to try a little experiment," he said, now resting his chin in one hand. "Our school promotes a program where students in the higher grades coach or tutor those in the lower grades. But we're going to do something different here."

I bit my bottom lip. What was he going to suggest?

"Shalini, you're probably my best math student," he said. "And you, Charlie, well—you're struggling."

Charlie looked down at his feet. I followed his gaze. One of his shoelaces had come undone.

"So I'm thinking, Shalini, that maybe you can help Charlie out. Be his tutor."

I froze on the spot. I had never even spoken to this boy and had no desire to after the way he had made my first day here a misery. I pulled the stack of books I was holding closer to my chest like a shield.

Charlie's head snapped in my direction and then back to Mr. Jeffries.

"What?" he snapped. "No way! I'm not having *her* anywhere near me." He said it as if I had leprosy. I hated him. It should have been me saying no. I was meant to be in AP Math. I shouldn't even be here.

Mr. Jeffries squared his gaze on Charlie, his eyes hardening.

"I don't really think you have a say in this," he said. "You're close to failing. If you want to have any chance of passing, you need the help of this young lady here. But if you have a better idea, I'd sure like to hear it."

Charlie glared at Mr. Jeffries for a second.

"Fine," he said under his breath, as if he were doing me a favor.

My heart sped, rage gathering in my belly. I was furious. I had no interest in helping this boy, and I was mad at Mr. Jeffries for just springing it on me. I had way too much work already. I decided I would tell him as much.

I opened my mouth, but the protests got stuck in my throat. The obedient girl kicked in again, the girl I had always been, the one who did what was asked of her.

"I will do my best to help, sir," I said quietly. I glanced over at Charlie. His face was sullen. His left cheek twitched nervously.

Charlie and I left the room together. We stood awkwardly in the hallway.

"So, like, what day?" he asked, looking right past me.

We settled on Wednesdays after school, in the library, for an hour. He tapped it into his phone, stuck the phone in his back pocket, turned around, and walked off.

A few days later, I found him waiting for me at a table in the farthest corner of the library. He barely looked up. I had been nervous about this all day. But now, looking down at him, I was just annoyed. An ache had started to form in my left temple. I sat in the chair across from him, staring at the pile of books that were scattered on the table. On the top was his most recent test paper, the one on which he had scored a D.

"Where are you having the most trouble?" I asked him. He shook his head and folded his arms across his chest.

"All of it," he said. "I don't see what the point is. I'm never gonna need any of this crap. I don't care."

"Look. If you want to pass the course, you have to care a little." My voice sounded impatient to my own ears. "You know, I have lots of other things I should be doing instead of being here. So if you really don't want to learn, tell me now so I won't waste my time." I was scarcely breathing. I couldn't believe the words were coming out of my mouth.

Charlie sat up straight and uncrossed his arms, like a child who had just been chastised at the dining table for playing with his food.

"Okay," he said.

"Good," I replied, pulling his books toward me.

"Now, let's start at the beginning,"

We went over the basics of perimeters and volumes. He had a decent grasp of some of the simpler concepts but had lost his way after that. By the end of the hour he seemed a little more confident, and I was a little more relaxed. Afterward, we stood at the top of the steps to the library. He looked a little off-balance, his backpack weighing him down on one side.

"Thanks," he said.

"You are welcome," I replied.

"See ya," he muttered, walking down the steps to a waiting car.

At home later, I emailed Vikram and told him about my new "student." Then I went upstairs to see Sangita. She was sitting on her bed doing homework, chewing on the back of a pencil. Her fingernails were painted bright blue. A Justin Bieber song was playing on the radio, and her right foot was tapping lightly to the music. There was so much about her I didn't recognize anymore.

"Hi, *didi*," she said when I walked in. "How did it go? With that rude boy?"

Her eyes opened wide when I told her how I had almost lost my temper with him, and she put her hands over her mouth.

"Good for you, *di*," she said. "Good that he saw he couldn't push you around anymore!" We both giggled. Then her face became more serious.

"Are you enjoying it here more now?" she asked. She cocked her head to one side, the way she often did when she asked a question.

"I suppose I am. Except for Ma. I'm still worried about her."

Sangita turned on her back. Her breathing became heavier. She had tears in her eyes.

"What? What is it?" I rushed to her side and put my arm around her skinny shoulders.

"I hate her," my sister said quietly.

"Who?"

"Ma. I hate her. I hate that she's in her stupid room all day. She doesn't care about us." She was sobbing now as I held her. I hadn't even considered how hard our mother's behavior had been on Sangita. She was still young and didn't understand the way my father and I were trying to.

"I'm sorry, *didi*," she said now, lifting her head and looking at me.

"It's okay. I know how you feel," I said. At that moment, I started to wonder what it would take to get my mother to be herself again. If we were sick, would she care for us? When our birthdays rolled around, would she bake us a cake, say a special morning prayer, smile proudly at how we had grown, kiss us on the foreheads like she had done every birthday for all our lives? What if she had retreated so far into a place that nothing—not even her love for us—could bring her back?

Fifteen

IN HOMEROOM, Mr. White started talking about a school-wide project that got my interest, the first time that had happened. Sangita had discovered swimming as a big love. I had yet to find mine. But when Mr. White started speaking now, I really listened. It might have been because he used the word *India* up front.

"The idea is to help women in developing countries: India, Bangladesh, Sri Lanka, Mexico," he said, scanning a flyer in his hand. "A new group called Food4Life, started by another eleventh grader to help underprivileged women start businesses, grow their own food, sustain their own lives." He turned the flyer around as if looking for any more pertinent information.

"Seems to be a worthwhile cause. If any of you has

the time, jump in. You can sign up here," he said, indicating a clipboard next to him. He put the flyer down on his desk on top of a pile of papers and tapped it as if indicating that he was done with that portion of homeroom.

Before leaving, I stood by his empty desk and picked up the clipboard. There were no other names on it. I took the pen attached to the clipboard but held it momentarily above the first line, where I should have been scribbling down my name. I really couldn't do this now. I had chores to take care of at home, a mother who needed tending to—the drugs hadn't worked, and she was no better. My father still had to be cooked for, and I had a fiancé thousands of miles away whom I missed. I had even offered to take home some of Charlie's math papers to look over after our weekly tutoring sessions. Charlie had said that polynomials and trig equations almost made sense now. Sometimes we would talk a little on the way out of the library. His father had found a new job, and things were better at home. At school, he'd mumble a "Hey" as I walked by. My father had seen the pressure I was under and briefly considered hiring a housekeeper. But he quickly changed his mind, realizing he wouldn't feel comfortable with someone he didn't know in the house all day and his wife too depressed to oversee what he would describe as "the running of the household."

Things were crazy enough. I needed to just bide my time for the next couple of years, not spread myself too thin.

But I loved the whole idea behind Food4Life. I liked what they were trying to do. I was reminded about how charity was such a big part of our home life in India. Dada was always willing to help out a struggling family, a cause, an organization that did good. It gave him immense satisfaction, and I had grown up seeing the value of being of service to others. Right now I remembered Renuka's advice to me. If I wanted to squeeze any joy out of my time here, I couldn't sit on the sidelines anymore.

I wrote down my name, email address, and phone number.

That evening I received a text from a girl named Amina, telling me that the first meeting was scheduled for the coming weekend at her house.

At eleven on the following Saturday morning, I nervously rang the doorbell as my father waited in the car until he saw that I'd been let in.

"Hey." The girl smiled, opening the door. "Shalini, right? I'm Amina." She wore big glasses that covered half her face, and her frizzy hair was pulled back into a tight ponytail. "Everyone else is already here. Come on in."

I followed her down a set of carpeted steps to a basement that had been transformed into kind of a den/study; there was a TV in one corner, a laptop computer in another, a minifridge, books everywhere, family pictures on the walls. It was cozy and welcoming, and I instantly felt at ease.

Three other people were seated around a coffee table. I found a spot and settled in.

"We were just about to get started," Amina said. "Let's quickly go around the room and say a little about ourselves and why we're here. I'll go first.

"Okay, so I'm Amina," she started. "I was born here, but my parents are from Bangladesh. I started Food4Life after reading an article about famine in Bangladeshi villages. I realized those families didn't need a handout but rather a way to make sure they were never hungry again. With this program, I want us to raise money to help women in as many underdeveloped countries as we can."

She turned to look at a pretty strawberry blonde next to her.

"Hey, I'm Justine," she said. "I'm on the cheerleading squad, I organize the regular school blood drive, and I am on the yearbook committee . . . so yeah, I really *need* to be doing something else." She rolled her eyes. We all chuckled. "But this seems really worthwhile, so I'm in."

Patrick, a tall, brown-haired boy, was next. He said he had already decided on a career with an NGO and thought this would give him a little hands-on experience. Catherine, a Korean girl, said she wanted to be able to "give back," and added that being involved in something like Food4Life would look great on her college applications.

Then it was my turn.

"My name is Shalini," I said. "I'm from India. I grew up witnessing poverty on a daily basis. I would give a few rupees here and there, but I knew it would not really make a difference. I feel that something like this, something that goes to the heart of a family, can really make an impact. I feel obliged to help."

Amina handed us each an orange folder containing sheets of paper with the Food4Life mission statement, one another's contact details, and a list of possible fundraising ideas.

"Wanna brainstorm?" she asked.

We were sitting on coffee-stained floral furniture, passing around a big bag of potato chips, cans of Pepsi and Sprite hissing softly as we opened them. Amina, a hand cupping her chin, looked over at me and smiled. I glanced around at the group, at these kids who seemed so, well, *nice*, and settled back into my comfy armchair. I might just have finally found a place where I belonged.

Vikram called very early on Valentine's Day, his cheery voice wishing me a "happy and lovely day!" He had already sent me an e-card: a picture of a woman with bright red fingernails holding a tiny red cardboard heart with a ribbon tied around it.

The words read: *My heart. It's yours.* It was very sweet, very Vikram.

"I've been missing you a lot," he said on the phone now. Lately people in India had been embracing Valentine's Day with new fervor, young people catching on that it was now something trendy to celebrate. For the past two years Vikram and I had exchanged home-made cards; and last year when he had come over for dinner with his family, he had brought me a single white rose, leading all my cousins to shout *"Wah re wah,"* which loosely translates as "Wow, oh, wow," while Dada shook his head disapprovingly.

"Have you been missing me?" he asked now.

"Of course I have," I said. "But I've been so busy with this new group."

Amina had stressed the importance of doing as much as we could in the four months left before the end of the school year. There had been a bake sale the previous week when Justine and I had set up a table on the school grounds during lunch break and sold cupcakes and peanut brittle. The preparation had taken my entire Sunday, for as well as I could cook Indian food, baking, I had discovered, was not my forte. Nobody had ever told me that you needed to let cupcakes cool before you iced them, or that there was a difference between baking soda and baking powder. I hadn't ever touched an egg before. The kitchen had been a disaster area, and I'd had flour in my hair for two days afterward. But sitting next to Justine behind a table selling sweet things for a dollar apiece, chatting during those quiet moments—I had just loved it. This past weekend, Patrick and I had organized a book drive, collecting unwanted books from students to sell. I'd had no idea how much work all of this would take but didn't regret joining for a second.

What I liked the most was that none of us had a specific "job"; we all pitched in, and so far everybody seemed to be doing an equal amount of work. I had printed out flyers, or had been in charge of the money, or had asked my father to help me set up a charity car wash down the street. We often lunched together in the cafeteria, talking not just about what we were going to do next for Food4Life, but about other parts of our lives as well:

Patrick flew gas-powered radio-controlled planes on weekends, Justine's parents were about to foster a young black kid from South Central, Catherine's older brother had been accepted into Harvard. I loved being included, becoming a part of their lives, a member of these new, interconnected circles.

I thought of all this when Vikram asked me if I missed him. I had been too preoccupied to really be missing anyone.

"School is so crazy, actually. I went from having nothing to do to having too much!"

"Well, Shalu, I told you," he said, "that you would find friends and be happy there. I knew it would happen. I wish I could be there with you, especially today."

I paused for a moment. There was a more expansive quality to my life now, more in it than ever before. And because of that, Vikram had a smaller role. It was weird to even think that, but it was true.

"I wish you could be here too," I said, a little preoccupied.

Mr. Jeremy invited my family out to dinner on our six-month anniversary in Los Angeles. He had asked Renuka and her parents to join us as well. As he always did before we went anywhere special, my father talked quietly to my mother, urging her again to please come along. She was on a new drug now, Dr. Gupta having explained to us that sometimes it was a question of trial and error before you had the right medication.

"Asha, half a year has passed," I heard my father say as we were preparing to leave. "You cannot continue this. We have all settled in here and are making very comfortable lives. Please, Asha, just snap out of it now."

"I'm not bothering you if I'm sitting here," my mother said, raising her voice slightly. "I'm not telling you not to go. I'm fine at home. You go, all of you. Just leave me alone."

My father appeared from the room, his face filled with frustration.

"I give up," he said, shaking his head.

"Papa, let me try," I said. I went in and sat on my mother's bed. She was twirling her *mangal sutra* with one finger.

"You're looking very nice," she said. I was wearing a long, flowing gray skirt and a red top with a cowl neck. It had become my new "best frock."

She looked up at me, her face shaded with sadness. She pulled me to her. Her hair was damp. She smelled of rosewater and jasmine, and a small dusting of talcum powder from the back of her neck rubbed off onto my top, leaving it speckled in white. It had been her first shower in five days.

"I will stay home with you," I said. "We will sit and watch TV together, and I will make you *chaat*."

"You don't need me," she said. "Nobody needs me. I am worthless here. Everybody is managing fine without me."

I opened my mouth to tell her she was wrong, but she silenced me with a finger to my lips.

"Daddy's boss has invited you. Please just go."

At the restaurant, I decided not to think about my mother. The evening was so much fun, and I didn't want anything to spoil it. Renuka, Sangita, and I sat at one end of the table, sipping Coke in frosted glasses. Renuka said my new outfit looked "sick," which I was given to understand is a good thing in Renuka-speak. We giggled about Vikram. Renuka asked if she could try on the ruby ring, and I let her. She held up her hand in front of her, clapped, and said, "Yay!" Then she covered her head with her napkin and pretended to be a blushing Hindu bride, and we giggled some more. When she gave me back the ring, she forced a pout and said, "Boo hoo." I gazed at the sparkling little ruby proudly.

Mr. Jeremy raised his glass of wine and toasted my

father, wishing him a "happy semi-anniversary," thanking him for his hard work. And my sweet father looked radiant with pride and joy. I so deeply wished my mother had been there to see it.

Sixteen

AS I WALKED THROUGH THE DOOR after school, my father was just ending a phone conversation with Dr. Gupta. He had scheduled another appointment. The doctor wanted to see how my mother was responding to the new medication.

"She thinks your mother needs therapy," my father said, rubbing his forehead. It was hard for him to get the words out. In his mind they symbolized family dysfunction, some great failure on his part to make his wife happy.

"Will she go?" I asked. The house was otherwise quiet. Sangita was with Amy at a swim meet.

"It will take a lot of convincing. It's hard enough to get her to see Dr. Gupta."

A few days later, I accompanied them back to the doctor's office. After half an hour, my father came out.

"There is nothing physically wrong with her, thank the Lord. The results of all her tests are normal." There had been a CBC, a thyroid function check, something else to determine the health of the kidneys and liver, tests to determine calcium and magnesium deficiencies. My mother had always been a strong, healthy woman. I hated that she was being treated like an invalid, that I knew the difference between Zoloft and Lexapro.

"So what then, Papa?" I asked.

"It's all in her head," he said a little uncharitably.

My mother stayed with the doctor for another twenty minutes or so. When she came out, she looked a little more relaxed. She sat down next to me, and my father went back in to speak with the doctor. When he was done, we all walked in silence to the car.

My mother fell asleep in the car on the way home. We had stopped at a red light. My father turned toward me, casting a quick eye toward my mother in the back to make sure she was fully asleep.

"Dr. Gupta has had some experience with these things," my father said. "She runs a support group for women from the subcontinent who have different problems. Marriage issues. Abuse. Whatever. It is more common than you know. They meet once every two weeks, there in her office. Women from our country. Women like your mother. The doctor thinks that maybe Asha will feel a kinship with some of the other women who come there. Perhaps someone who knows what she is going through. She thinks there is a good chance there will be progress."

I thought for a moment about what my father was saying. In the end, maybe my mother needed a bit of what I'd found recently: a place to fit in, with people she could relate to. It wouldn't hurt to try.

The light turned green. We sped home.

Charlie and I stood outside the library after our study hour, our sixth together.

"You've really helped me," he said. "You explained it in a way I could understand." The sun's rays glinted off the silver studs on a black wrist cuff he always wore, and his usually gel-spiked hair looked tamer today.

"So I'm good," he said. "I mean, I don't want to take up any more of your time. I think I'll do okay on the final. You got me through a rough spot." He looked down at the ground, kicking a tiny rock.

"In that case, I'm very glad I could be of help," I said, smiling broadly. "Should you ever require my assistance again, you know where to find me."

"Listen," Charlie said, looking at me now. "In the beginning, when you first got to school, I was a real douche. I'm sorry."

"Yes, my feelings were hurt," I said. "But what is important is that you are no longer a douche."

We both laughed.

That evening Amina called me at home, sounding as rushed as she usually did.

"The stuff we've been doing so far has been great; we've made some money, but we kinda need to up the stakes a bit," she said.

"What are you thinking?" I asked.

"There's a school orchestra; it's really great, one of the best in the region. They've been invited all over the place to perform. I think last year they even went to Mexico."

"And?" I asked hurriedly. I had been about to go give my mother her meds.

"I'm thinking we can see if they might consider doing a concert for us. We could sell tickets, and all the proceeds could go to Food4Life. We could make a chunk of change if we fill the auditorium."

Some of the orchestra members were going to be in regular practice the following afternoon. Amina asked me to meet her at the auditorium.

She and I were the only people sitting in the darkened empty audience section of the auditorium. There were just a handful of performers, each playing a solo while the others offered critiques. There was a long-haired Asian girl with thin arms pounding on the keys of a grand piano. Then came a few kids on the violin, viola, and cello, all playing skillfully. After they finished, a tousled-haired boy blew through a French horn, and someone next to him played a gleaming trumpet.

"They're great, aren't they?" Amina whispered.

"Yes, I guess," I responded. I knew very little about music and had nothing to compare this to. But it all sounded very professional.

Amina's eyes scanned the stage. "There's a student orchestra liaison guy. Don't think he's here yet. He's the guy who works things out between the players and the conductor. We need to talk to him."

A latecomer rushed in through a side door and quickly unpacked a silver flute from a black case. He waited till the trumpeter was finished and then put his flute to his lips.

I couldn't take my eyes away from him. It might have been the distraction of him coming in so late, rustling the pages of his music book on the stand in front of him.

Or it might have been how he played. The music from his flute alternated between soft and mellow, high and piercing. His fingers breezed along his sparkling instrument. His head, topped by a soft mop of black hair, bounced in tune with the music as if it was coming from his whole body instead of just his lips. I was fixated, hearing him and nothing else, nothing more than the magnificence of the music that resounded off these walls, seeing nothing more than a boy with a gray T-shirt and faded black jeans, his eyes closed, his head lilting in time to his own music. All I could see through the empty rows in front of us, past the diffused illumination from the spotlights overhead, was him, a modern-day Krishna with his flute.

Amina, Patrick, and I sat on a blanket under a thick oak tree, its branches overhanging, waiting. She had arranged to meet with orchestra members who were interested in helping out with the concert. Amina had told me that the boy with the flute was the "go-to" guy. The conductor, also the head of the music department, was too busy to get involved on a day-to-day basis. The flute guy was the buffer between the orchestra members and the rest of the school. If the concert was going to happen, it would happen on his say-so.

I felt a little thrill at the thought of seeing him again.

I couldn't comprehend it, but I had thought of little else since seeing him play. After I had left the auditorium, my legs were wobbling and I was sweating. I'd wondered who he was, what year he was in, why I had never noticed him before. I had shaken my head to dislodge those thoughts of him, thoughts that should have been reserved for my Vikram. This flute-playing boy had no right to be there.

A small group approached: I recognized the thin Asian pianist, a cellist, a boy at the back who had played the drums. And walking behind them, smiling as he talked to one of his companions, was the flute player.

Patrick began making the introductions. I blanked out when the musicians were telling us their names. The only name I heard was Tobias.

"But call me Toby," he said, grinning. "I suppose I'm kinda in charge. I brought along some other players to help make a decision. So, what are we doing?"

Toby was sitting three people down from me. I leaned forward to look at him. Up close he was even nicer looking than he had been onstage. His black hair came to below his ears, long in the back and swept to one side at the top, covering his forehead. His eyes were a deep, dark brown. He was wearing jeans and a white T-shirt with a large graphic of a silver-winged motorcycle on the front. He had on a thin white jacket. When he smiled, a small dimple appeared in his right cheek.

"Well, here's the plan," said Amina. "We want you to put on a concert that we'd sell tickets to. We're thinking maybe in six weeks? Enough time to get the word out, but not too close to the craziness of finals and prom. This is going to be our biggest fund-raiser of the year, so we really need it to work. What do you guys think?"

Toby looked at the group.

"Well?" he asked. "Are we in?"

Everyone nodded.

"I'll talk to the rest of the orchestra, but I don't see why not," Toby said finally.

Amina punched her fist in the air and looked around at us.

I was thrilled too. But for an entirely different reason.

"Holy crap, you have a crush!" Renuka said in typically understated Renuka-speak. "That is wicked funny!"

We were on the phone, and she couldn't stop laughing. I was now questioning the wisdom of having called her.

"I knew that even *you* wouldn't be able to resist," she said, her giggling fit thankfully subsided. "There are way too many hot guys in high school. I'm just shocked it's taken you this long."

"Renuka, I'm *engaged*," I said, stating the obvious. "I have a boy in Bangalore waiting for me. What am I doing even thinking about another boy?"

"Yeah, yeah, you're engaged. Blah blah blah," she said. "But you haven't seen the dude in months; and he's, like, nine *thousand* miles away. You know, just because you like a new boy here doesn't mean you're doing anything wrong. You're not going to run off and marry him. You just like a boy. Don't get all freaked out about it. He probably has a girlfriend anyway."

I didn't like hearing that. Not one little bit. Ever since that meeting on the grass two days earlier, Toby had been my perpetual imaginary companion. As I made dinner, I wondered what he was doing at that precise moment. As I served my father *jalebis*, I wondered if Toby liked Indian desserts. I had searched for him on the Valley Crest Youth Orchestra page to see if anything came up. I called Amina and tactfully fished for information. She was way too immersed in her busy life to think too much about it. But at least I found out a couple of things: he was a senior, had been playing the flute since he was four, and was considered something of a prodigy. She said that on his Facebook page he mentioned that he hoped to get into Juilliard.

Renuka was right: this *was* a crush, based on what

I had read in teen novels and seen on TV shows. I just really, really liked this boy. I liked the way he spoke, how he looked, how kind his face was, and how beautifully he played. Something about him reminded me of Vikram.

Vikram! I banged my palm against my head as if doing so would crush these terrible, disloyal thoughts. What of Vikram? My betrothed and my intended? Was I even *allowed* to be thinking of another boy? What would my parents say? And his? And, worst of all, Dada?

I took a big, deep breath. "This is ridiculous," I said to myself out loud. "This boy is nothing to you. Get him out of your head. Stop all this silly daydreaming. You have to get it together."

Seventeen

WHAT HAPPENED NEXT reminded me of Dada's favorite saying: "Man proposes; God disposes," which essentially means that people can plan anything they want, but sometimes life has something else in mind.

I had resolved to stay firmly focused on the task at hand: helping Amina organize and sell tickets to a concert to raise money to help women in remote Nepalese villages learn how to read. It seemed pretty straightforward. And it was—until Amina made yet another request of me.

"Listen," she said, cornering me as I rummaged through my locker. By now I knew that when she started a sentence with "Listen," she would be asking me to go above and beyond the call of duty.

"You know how with the previous stuff we've done everybody kind of pitched in and helped out, right? Well, we need to be a bit more organized this time. Each one of you guys in the group will have a task or, like, a few tasks."

"Okay," I said, slamming my locker shut. "I can get posters printed and put them up, maybe organize for a concession stand on the night of the concert? Bring some extra money in?"

"Yeah, yeah, all good," said Amina. Like me, she was rushing to get to her next class.

"But a bit more than that. You know how Toby is kind of the liaison guy at the orchestra, right?" she asked. The mention of his name made me stiffen my back. "Well, I need you to do the same for us. You basically need to liaise with Toby. If an orchestra member has a question or problem, they go to him, he goes to you, you come to me. You make sure the musicians have everything they need on the night of the concert. Basically, get what Toby says the group needs. Sort of the go-between between them and us. Cool?"

My immediate instinct was to say no, because doing what Amina asked would require me to be in close proximity to Toby; and proximity to him wasn't something I needed right now. But what reason could I give her— especially when I had so enthusiastically volunteered my time and support during our earliest meetings? How could I backtrack now?

Still, it was worth a shot.

"Um, you know, Amina, maybe I should focus on some of the other things, like selling tickets. You could ask Catherine instead. I think she knows more about music than I do." I realized how feeble I sounded.

"Oh, please," said Amina, turning to walk away. "You can totally do it. Text him. Just get going on it, okay?" And off she went.

I stood there leaning against my locker. I could do this. I would just be professional, composed, controlled. I knew how to be all those things. I wouldn't let this throw me. I had a fiancé.

The bell rang, and I rushed to class.

I texted Toby that evening, although I must have written and rewritten the message on a scrap of paper a dozen times before I actually punched the letters into my phone.

"Hey," I wrote. "It's Shalini from Food4Life. Amina said to connect. See what u need 4 ur group." All the abbreviations went against my formal and somewhat perfectionist nature, but thanks to Renuka, it felt as if I'd learned a whole new language.

He texted back almost immediately.

"Gr8," he wrote. "Let's talk tmrw after school, outside. I'll find u."

Throughout preparing dinner, taking a tray up to my mother, folding a pile of laundry that had sat in a basket for four days, and wiping down the stove, I thought only of Toby. I began counting the hours until I would be able to talk to him after school. I figured it would just be a quick conversation. But those three words were imprinted on my brain: *I'll find u.* Tomorrow afternoon, Toby—by far the cutest and sweetest boy in the entire school—was going to come find me. I sighed deeply, left my father in front of the TV and Sangita at the dining table finishing her homework, and went upstairs to pick up my mother's tray.

I knocked on the door.

"Shalu?" she called out. I opened the door and went inside. The plates on the tray were almost empty.

"The *dal* was especially good today," she said. "You and your sister are becoming very good cooks."

"Thanks, Ma," I replied. "I'm so happy you're eating properly."

"Come, sit," she said, making a spot for me on the bed. Her eyes looked a little brighter. It might have been the fact that she had eaten well for once, or perhaps it was the new drugs she was on. I felt a little heartened.

Maybe my mother was finally coming back.

"Kalpana could finally be with Mohit," my mother said dreamily.

"Sorry, Ma?" I was confused. I didn't know any Kalpana or any Mohit, and I was sure she didn't either.

"There," she said, pointing to the TV screen. I turned to look. The credits for a popular Hindi soap opera were rolling.

"They were so much in love, but too many things stood in their way. They couldn't be together. But just now, finally, he found her and they married." She had a look of pure contentment on her face.

My heart sank. She was talking about fictional characters on a TV show. She was still in her dark, unreachable place, emerging only to check in on the lives of people who didn't even exist.

Holding back the tears, I kissed her good night, picked up the tray, and left the room.

The next morning Toby was the first thing that popped into my head. Only eight hours and he and I would be chatting on the stairs outside the school, maybe standing aside from everyone else engaged in a private, meaningful conversation.

I had decided, somewhere between last night and this

morning, that it was okay for me to look forward to it. My mother had her escapist fantasy, wanting to live in some nonexistent TV world. And perhaps it would be okay for me to dream too. Maybe Renuka was right; I wasn't committing any crime. I still loved Vikram; he was always going to be the boy I would marry. In eighteen months he and I would be together again. But in the meantime, just as my mother couldn't control her depression, I couldn't control the fact that I liked another boy. I just knew that I would never, ever do anything about it. And I knew that once the concert was over I would go back to my own life and would have nothing to do with him again. And then the feeling would just fade.

While Sangita was in the shower, I tried on a few different outfits, leaving in a pile on my bed my old clothes from India, my new ones from Target, and a few things that Renuka had let me have. I was looking for the hippest, most current one, which was a long shot in my still-limited wardrobe. I would have loved Sangita's opinion—she seemed to have the whole fashion thing nailed, even if she was only eleven. But I didn't want her to see me obsess over something as trivial as clothes. She knew that wasn't me.

I finally settled on a pair of navy blue cords, a light blue long-sleeved T-shirt, and a denim jacket. I put the sparkly clip in my hair and threw on some flat ankle boots I had bought with Renuka one day. I looked at myself in the mirror from a dozen different angles and had to concede that I looked pretty good.

I stopped in to see my mother before going down for breakfast. My father was almost ready, weaving a belt through the loops on his pants. My mother was still asleep. My father said she had been up all night, finally falling asleep at dawn.

"Let her rest," he whispered. "This evening is the first meeting at Dr. Gupta's. Remember, I told you?"

In all the craziness of the past couple of weeks, I had completely forgotten my mother's support group session.

"Of course I remember," I lied.

He mumbled about not being able to find his comb and went back into the bathroom to look for it. I was about to turn around and go out when I caught sight of a gold lipstick case on the dressing table. I reached out for it, uncovered it, swiveled the tube so a shimmering pink color came up. My mother and I had bought this together in Bangalore right before we had left. The lipstick was almost untouched. I looked at her sleeping form. She wouldn't mind me borrowing it. I slipped it into my pants pocket and left the room.

The door to the temple room was ajar. By the incense

burning there I could tell that Sangita had already been in. I slipped off my boots and went inside. I lit another stick of incense and circled it around all the statues, saying prayers beneath my breath: "Bless and protect my family. Bless and protect Vikram and his family. Please make my mother better. Please." My hand stopped in front of the Krishna statue and lingered there for a second. A tiny smile flickered across my face as I anticipated the day ahead.

As soon as the last class of the day ended, I rushed to the bathroom. I fished out a brush from my bag and ran it through my hair, unclipping and re-clipping my sparkling crescent moon barrette. I washed my hands and sprinkled a little water on my face, using my slightly damp fingers to push my eyelashes back so they would look curlier, a technique I had read about in some teen magazine at Renuka's house. It didn't work. I pinched my cheeks to bring in some color. That didn't work either. Finally, I pulled out my mother's lipstick tube from my pocket. I barely turned it, just enough so I could reach the surface of the lipstick with my finger. I dabbed a spot of the shiny pink wax onto my index finger and rubbed it on my lips. Then I pursed my lips together, checked my braces to make sure there was nothing stuck there, stood back for one last look, and ran outside.

Toby was standing against a wall, one leg bent up against it, his hair partially covering his face as he checked his phone. His flute case rested at his feet.

"Hi," I said, coming up to him.

He looked up and smiled. My stomach did a little flip.

"Hey," he said. "Wanna go sit over there?" He motioned to a stone bench.

We wove our way through the crowds of kids leaving.

We sat down. He stretched out his legs. I'd forgotten how tall he was. His teeth were very white and nearly perfect, and he smelled like spearmint. He shook his head slightly, moving the hair that fell into his eyes. "So, what's up?"

I froze. Since yesterday I had thought of nothing else but seeing him again, talking to him alone. But right now I blanked on what I was supposed to say.

"Oh, right," I said, collecting my thoughts. "Well, Amina, you know, thought that I should be your contact person. You know, if you or the other performers need anything from us. And that, you know, if I have to check something, I can come to you." I couldn't believe how many times I had said "you know." I wanted to kick myself.

"Sounds like a plan," he said. "I've locked in the date with the music department. Most of the other kids are on board, even if it adds a little more rehearsal time to their schedules. Everyone gets that it's a good cause. We're gonna repeat a concert we did in Seattle last year. A set of classical symphonies, concertos, duets, a couple of solos . . ."

He went on. I stared at how his lips moved when he talked, the way he stared right into my eyes.

". . . it ran about ninety minutes, with an intermission. I can email over the details so you can start working on the programs. Other than that, we're good to go."

He spoke quickly, clearly, taking charge. In addition to him being supercute and a fantastic flutist (from what I could tell in my limited experience of flutists), he was obviously really smart as well. There was no way my crush was going away anytime soon.

He stood up.

"I gotta go get my little sister from soccer practice. So, we'll talk, yeah?" He, like me, had a younger sister; *and* he was picking her up? What a kind brother he was! Could he be more perfect?

"I like your flute," I blurted, feeling instantly stupid afterward. "You know, it's silver."

I needed to shut up now.

Toby grinned.

"Um, thanks," he said. "But they're pretty much always silver." He smiled again, turned around, and left.

I sat on the bench for a few minutes. Part of me was exhilarated; he was just so *nice*. Another part of me was embarrassed at my stupid comments. "I like your flute?" I couldn't have come up with anything smarter?

But it didn't matter. The exhilaration outweighed the embarrassment. Sitting there on the hard stone bench, watching kids stream past me, I decided that for the first time since I got to this country I was going to let myself have a little fun.

There was crying and hollering coming from the master bedroom.

"Asha, you have to come with me; this is not negotiable," my father said sternly. I could hear everything through the open door.

"I'm not interested in going and talking to a bunch of women I don't know!" my mother shouted, crying. "Stop asking me to do it. I won't!"

I stood at the doorway. My father's face was red, his fists clenched at his side.

"Papa, can I help?" I asked.

My mother wiped her tears with the back of her hand. She was chewing her hair. She was unkempt. She looked like she was on the edge of going crazy. When did things get so bad?

My father stalked off. My mother flopped onto the bed, and I lay next to her. She was a sliver of her former self, slight and frail, joyless. She was breathing heavily.

"I know I'm sick," she said to me, her voice almost a whisper.

I stared at her. This was the first time she had acknowledged what the rest of us knew.

"Of course I know. I am always sad, crying, mad. I hate everyone. Even your father. But not you, Shalu. Never you and Sangita. You are my only reason for living. If you weren't here, I would have left this earth already. Believe me, I have thought of it."

"Ma . . ." I was weeping. That she was in so much pain that she had considered suicide was more hurtful to me than I could bear.

"I know I am sick. I don't know how to get better," she said.

"Ma, do you want to get better?" I asked. Strands of damp black hair clung to her sallow skin.

"For you," she said. "I want to be better for you."

"Then please, let Papa take you to the meeting. It will be a start. Just one time; and if you don't like it, nobody will ask you to go back."

Her red eyes landed on mine.

"Please." I sounded like a little girl at a carnival

pleading for another pony ride. I was desperate.

Almost imperceptibly, she nodded.

My father said that what happened behind the closed doors of Dr. Gupta's office was a mystery to him. When he realized he wouldn't be granted access to the inner sanctum—a room populated by several women of various South Asian cultures and, from his estimation, ranging in age from twenty-five to sixty—he had told the receptionist he would be back to pick up my mother in an hour and strolled down to the nearest Coffee Bean for an overpriced iced *chai* drink.

Once home, my mother had gone straight upstairs to bed, although she had bent down to kiss my forehead, a gesture that reminded me of her healthier self.

"In the car, she said thank you to me," said my father. "This must be a good sign, no?"

"How'd it go?" Amina asked me at school the next day. She had chased me down the hallway as I went from one class to the next. Looking at her, I spaced out for a second. I had been so preoccupied with my mother and getting her to the support group the previous evening that I had come down off my high after my little chat with Toby.

"The meeting with Toby?" Amina prompted me. She

liked to describe everything as meetings, even if it was a couple of kids sitting on a park bench for all of three minutes.

"Toby was great," I said, beaming. "Um, I mean, the meeting was great." I recounted what he'd told me, that on the music end, everything was planned.

"So all we have to do is wait for the details—the titles of the songs they'll be playing—and we can print the programs," I said. "In the meantime we should get some flyers ready and start preselling tickets."

Over lunch, we sat clustered around a corner table with our orange folders and scratch paper, eating and brainstorming. Patrick went to fetch more water; Catherine checked her emails on her phone. A few months ago I'd been eating alone. Now I was lunching with a group of people I felt a real kinship with. That in itself made me happy.

Patrick said he'd put up a Facebook page for the event. We talked about the viability of having a snack bar and seeing who could sponsor food that we could sell. We talked about ticket prices and maybe offering some sort of child care on the night of the concert so families with younger children could come too. We tried to cover everything. Catherine sketched out what the flyers would look like: "A Night of Classics" and then underneath: "Valley Crest Youth Orchestra and Food4Life present an evening of fine music. All proceeds to go to fund women's literacy in Nepal." Then Amina quibbled for a few minutes about our organization getting second billing.

"It was our idea," she said, meaning it was actually *her* idea. "We went to *them*, not the other way around."

"Fine," said Catherine, transposing the names of the orchestra and the charity. "Don't think it makes that much of a difference, but whatever you say."

We all looked at it. Even sketched in pencil on a sheet of lined A4 paper, it had a clean, professional appearance.

True to his word, Toby emailed me later that day with the list of pieces the orchestra was planning on playing. The names meant nothing to me: Danse Infernale— *The Firebird Suite* by Igor Stravinsky, Vivaldi's Concerto Grosso in D Minor—Spring from *The Four Seasons*, Piano Solo—"Flight of the Bumblebee" by Nikolai Rimsky-Korsakov. European classical music was a whole other world. It was never played at home in Bangalore or something I'd learned about in school. I don't think I'd ever even heard a sampling of it—something that, at this particular moment, filled me with a considerable amount of embarrassment.

As soon as I'd finished reading his note, an email popped up from Vikram. Seeing their names in my in box, one directly beneath the other, made me feel a bit sick.

"Hi Shalu," Vikram wrote. "What's going on? Haven't heard from you in a while. How are Uncle? Aunty? And Sangita? And school? Everything really good here. Busy with finals. Lots and lots of work. I'll call you in the morning, okay? Love you lots, Vikram."

Somehow, I didn't feel as excited to hear from Vikram. And then it hit me. It was almost identical to every other email he'd sent me since I'd been here. It was sweet and affectionate. But he asked me about the same things he always did—my parents and sister—and told me about the same things he always did—college and his busy life. There was no mention of Stravinsky, or fundraisers, or the most worthwhile charities to support. Not that there should have been, of course. But everything about Toby was new and interesting, and everything about Vikram was the same as it had always been: cozy, kind . . . and the same. I hated feeling that way. But there it was.

Toby texted me before dinner.

"Did u get my email? All ok?"

"xlnt," I wrote back. "Repertoire looks good." (Not that I'd know the difference.)

"Need to go over a few things," he wrote. "Lunchtime Monday?"

161

Eighteen

EVEN THOUGH, technically speaking, Toby hadn't asked me out to lunch, I spent the weekend happily deluding myself that he had done just that. Despite my limited experience with such things, even I knew that there was a definite difference between being asked to go to lunch with someone and meeting them at lunchtime. But I liked the idea that Toby had asked to see me at a time when he was no doubt busy and in demand. There was going to be food involved. It would, most likely, be just the two of us. This was as close to a "lunch date" with him as I would ever get.

We had arranged to meet on the lawn by the big oak tree.

On Monday morning I could barely think about

anything else; homeroom, math, English—it was all a blur, me just going through the motions. It wasn't in character for me. But this whole thing—my infatuation with this boy—was very out of character for me as well.

At the appointed time I rushed over to the meeting place. He wasn't there yet. I wondered if he might have a picnic basket and a blanket, if we would be like all those other kids who relaxed on the grounds at lunchtime, eating sandwiches and salads from plastic containers. We would have an interesting and funny conversation, and maybe I would see something in his eyes telling me he felt about me like I felt about him. I smoothed down my hair and took a book from my bag, pretending to look casual, but I couldn't concentrate on a single word.

I looked up after a few moments and saw him crossing the grounds toward me. He was with two girls. My heart sank. There was no picnic basket, and he was bringing friends. Maybe one was his girlfriend, I realized. The thought alone made me nauseous.

He stopped for a second, said something to the girls; they looked my way, nodded smilingly, and hung back. He strolled alone toward me. My heart rose a little.

"Hey," he said, tossing his hair away from his eyes. "Sorry I'm a couple of minutes late."

"It's okay," I said, tucking my book back into my bag.

163

"Shall we sit somewhere?"

"I can't really stay," he said. "I just needed to give you this."

My heart sank again. This wasn't what I had hoped it would be. From a folder in his backpack he pulled out the orchestral seating plan for the night of the concert.

"It's pretty self-explanatory," he said. "We'll have it all set up the night before. But I wanted you to have a copy of it just in case anything comes up, if one of the musicians is sick or something and we have to make some last-minute adjustments onstage."

"Oh," I said. "Cool."

"That's it," he said. His thumb was hooked through a belt loop. He stared at me through feathery-dark lashes. He was so good-looking, it kind of took my breath away. "Oh, we'll need bottled water backstage at intermission. The theater department knows how to do the lighting. It's all good. If you think of anything else, text me. I'll do the same. But for now, that's it. Gotta run," he said.

"Okay," I said, cursing myself for my pathetic monotone responses.

He turned and went off, rejoining the group, leaving me standing by the oak tree, yesterday's squashed sandwich at the bottom of my bag.

Even though I was fully cognizant of the fact that I

had set myself up for this disappointment, I felt utterly dejected the rest of the day. I had allowed myself to think that this lunch meeting with Toby was going to be a big deal, that it would be some insanely romantic interlude in an otherwise ordinary day. Instead, he had handed me a sheet of paper and within thirty seconds had returned to a far more attractive and radiant group of people. Who could blame him?

There was something different about the couch when I got home that evening. The four cushions that usually lay on it were now propped up, their pointed velvet corners touching. I squinted at them.

My mother. This was how she always arranged cushions. She had been down here. This was her handiwork.

A surge of excitement swept through me. I leaped upstairs, rushing past the temple room from where I could smell freshly lit incense. She had been in there too. Somewhere between last night and this morning, my mother—my drug-addled, depressed, dependent mother—had come back to us. My heart cheered.

She was in my bedroom folding T-shirts. She turned to look at me as I stood in the doorway, my hands clutching the frame. There was a lightness to her face.

"Has Sangita gone swimming?" she asked. She had

noticed my sister's stronger, tanned body, strands of her dark hair burnished by the sun. "With her new friend?"

"Yes, Ma. Amy. Her best friend." I let my arms drop.

"Good. Friends are important," she said.

She and I stood in silence. I wanted to ask her about the night before, to ask her how she was feeling, what she was going through. But I was scared to disrupt the calm that seemed to have settled over us.

"Your clothes are folded," she said. "I'm feeling a headache coming on. I need to lie down."

She went into her bedroom and gently shut the door.

She did not come out of her room again for the next four days.

Nineteen

THE TWO WEEKS BEFORE the concert were a blur.

My mother went to her second support group and was on her third set of drugs. My father still didn't know what went on inside the room, although he had spoken to the elderly father of another woman in the group who had said he felt that all the women there "just complained." Dr. Gupta would only say that progress was being made, that the forum would provide a place where my mother would "feel safe," as if she was in any danger at home. My father was simply grateful that my mother would leave the confines of her room at least once every two weeks, although he had to concede that there were instances when her mood seemed lighter, that she said more than a few terse words in the course of the day.

But I still had heaps of household chores to deal with, a huge amount of homework, a fiancé I needed to try and speak with at least a couple of times a week. There were days when I would walk with Sangita to school in the morning and not see her again until bedtime. Then there was the obsession with a flute-playing boy that wouldn't release me. I couldn't stop thinking about Toby. Renuka said that I was "totally allowed to be crushing on him" and that it didn't make me bipolar, which was a relief.

Amina, in the meantime, had piled extra tasks on the group in preparation for the big show. She said we needed to be "relentless" about selling tickets. Mr. White announced the concert in homeroom a couple of times, and afterward a few of the kids—including Charlie—came up to me and bought a few tickets. Magali took four, and even smiled weakly at me and said thank you as she handed over the money for them. I was also responsible for arranging the concession booth; a local store had sponsored a refreshment table; and I had managed to convince Delhi Delites & Supplies to donate boxes of Indian snacks, which we could sell to make extra money.

Eight days before the concert, Amina called me in a panic. Not all the tickets had been sold. The auditorium was still half empty.

"I can put up more posters," I offered. "I'm sure that will help?"

"It's not looking good," she said. She sounded on the verge of tears. She had had such high hopes for the event, and she was taking personally the fact that the concert was not going to be sold out.

But then, three days later, she called again.

"We're at full house!" she shrieked. "Someone called and bought the rest of the tickets! It's crazy!" She was ecstatic.

The night before the concert I couldn't sleep. I had weird dreams of baby Krishna curled up in his mother's arms, flutes that danced in the air as if suspended from invisible strings, Vikram's face in the rain, Amina and me on a carousel ride. It was all nonsense, and I put it down to nerves. But I woke up tired. I wanted to stay in bed a little longer, but I had promised Amina that I would be at the school grounds by ten to oversee preparations.

It was a beautiful, sunny Saturday, the kind of day for which Los Angeles is famous. I made my way straight to the auditorium, which we had asked the night janitor to leave unlocked. I turned on all the lights, and they came on with startling brightness. The stage floor had been waxed to a shiny gloss; the music stands and chairs were already set up. I pulled out the seating chart Toby had given me and checked that everything was in order, counting the chairs and how many were in each row. It was perfect.

I walked back down the stairs to the seating area and up and down the aisles. The dark red carpet had been vacuumed, the armrests between seats cleaned, the wooden floors underneath swept. It looked as if nothing had been missed. But when I got to the last three rows, I noticed a couple of empty plastic water bottles littering the floor, a takeout bag, an old magazine, chewing gum wrappers. I wasn't sure what had happened there—maybe the janitor had to leave suddenly or had forgotten to do the back. I left the hall and found the room where the janitorial supplies were kept, grateful that the door was unlocked. I dragged a long, unwieldy broom and dustpan to the auditorium. I began sweeping the floor at the back of the room, making sure to check under the seats and in each armrest for old cups and used ticket stubs.

I was startled to hear the doors open. I looked up and saw that a few of the musicians were coming in. I checked my watch. I had forgotten that there was going to be an eleven o'clock rehearsal. Toby was leading the group. At first none of them saw me. They went up onstage, finding their places, laughing among themselves. I stood, leaning against the broom, watching. I couldn't take my eyes off Toby.

A girl with a harp was the first to see me.

"Oh, hey," she said. She was still holding her giant instrument. I wondered how she had gotten it here.

Everyone turned to see who she was talking to. I had put on my oldest clothes this morning, not thinking I'd run into anyone. My hair was in a ponytail coiled at the top of my head. I must have looked a sight.

"The janitor forgot to do these last three rows," I said. My voice rebounded off the walls in the quiet room. "I'll be done in a few minutes and then I'll be out of your way." I let go of the handle of the dustpan, and it clattered loudly to the floor. I bent down to pick it up and then accidentally let go of the broom. I couldn't believe how nervous I was.

Toby smiled, put down his flute case, and came bouncing down the steps.

"Here, let me help," he said. He walked toward me. He picked up the dustpan and broom.

"Who'd they make these for?" he asked. "LeBron James? Jeez, they're huge!" We both laughed. He swept while I bent over to pick up any trash, which seemed easier than dealing with the broom and dustpan. When everything looked in order, I told him I would take the equipment back to the cleaning closet and he could get on with the rehearsal.

"Thanks for helping," I said.

"No problem," he replied, his hands on his waist. "I want this to be a good night too. Not going to happen if someone smells last week's KFC under their seat." We laughed again. The lights overhead were positioned right on his dark, shiny hair. He smiled his bright smile. His eyelashes curled up just so. I was crazy about him.

After I left the auditorium, I saw Amina, Patrick, Justine, and Catherine in the foyer. They were unfolding large tables, tacking up posters, and removing stacks of programs from cardboard boxes. Amina said she could barely sleep the previous night, and the others seemed preoccupied and nervous. I could understand why: we had each invested so much time in this event. It belonged to all of us. We needed it to be a success.

"What are you smiling about?" Amina asked me. I was unfurling a banner for the refreshment stand. After my exchange just now with Toby, and flush with the warmth I felt that he so gallantly came over to help me sweep, I had a smile from ear to ear.

"Oh, nothing," I said. "Excited about tonight, that's all." Just my saying that seemed to reassure everyone.

We busied ourselves for the next few hours, unpacking

bottles of water and cans of soda and setting out snacks, putting up a booth for will-call and another table with a small cash box on top for selling programs. As soon as we did as much as we could, Amina offered to drive me home so I could shower and change.

I put on a silk tunic and matching pants. It was pink with silver embroidery, and I paired it with silver slippers, dangling earrings, and a dab of lip gloss. I stepped back and stared at myself in the mirror, happy with how I looked. This was the first time I was going to be "going ethnic" at school, which was how Amina described it; she was going to wear a sari. She said it would be in keeping with the spirit of the event. But I didn't need to be cajoled. I loved dressing like this on special occasions, and tonight was a special occasion. It was part of who I was, and I embraced the opportunity to step out in something that reflected my culture.

While I waited for Amina and her parents to pick me up, I packed up the boxes of Indian snacks that the owner of Delhi Delites had dropped off. Everything smelled and looked delicious, and I was sure they would be a welcome treat in addition to the potato chips, pretzels, cookies, and cupcakes we were selling.

"Papa, here are the tickets," I said, handing over three.

"Make sure you are there by six forty-five. We start at seven."

"Why are there three?" he asked. "It's just Sangita and me."

I looked down, a little ashamed. His face softened.

"You are still thinking your mother might come," he said. "I'm sorry, *beta*. This is all so hard on you. But she has not left the room since morning. I have told her a dozen times about today. But sometimes I don't think she even hears me."

I was fighting tears. I still prayed that my mother would suddenly snap out of it, that she would go back to being herself and would stay herself forever. Even if that was unrealistic, it was my biggest hope.

Amina honked outside.

"I'd better go," I said to my father. He looked like he wanted to hug me, but didn't. He had never been comfortable showing affection.

"Yes, *beta*, I'll see you at the show."

The school was still quiet when we arrived. Now that we were so close to the event, I was so nervous that my stomach actually ached. I couldn't even imagine how Amina felt. All the way over here in the car she was quiet, pulling nervously on her bottom lip. Even though we had all contributed so much time and energy, Food4Life was still her baby. If tonight was a failure, I knew she'd blame herself. I felt a sudden burst of sympathy for her.

Once at the school, Amina disappeared, and I busied myself arranging the rest of the snacks I had brought and putting out a price list. I made sure there were enough paper napkins, straws, and paper cups, and extra supplies beneath the table. Patrick was going around double-checking that everything was in place, while Justine and Catherine, who had volunteered as ushers for the night, were in the restroom putting on identical red shirts and black pants and name badges. In the back of my mind, I kept hoping to see Toby, but I knew I wouldn't; he and the rest of the orchestra would have gone straight to the stage via a back door. I had butterflies in my stomach just thinking of him.

The hall in front of the auditorium slowly started to fill. I noticed lots of familiar faces. Some of my teachers, the principal, Sasha and Magali with their parents, who were as good-looking as their daughters, were there. Charlie came in pushing a lady in a wheelchair. She was beautiful, with short, dark hair and pale skin. He came up to my table, where I was selling programs.

"Hey," he said, handing over some money. "This is my mom."

She reached up to hold my hand. It was an affectionate

gesture. I never expected him to have a mother in a wheelchair. Seeing him now behind her, taking care of her, humanized him even more.

"I'm so happy to meet you," she said, squeezing my fingers. "Charlie's told me so much about you, about how you helped him. I'm very grateful." She smiled at me.

"It was my pleasure, ma'am," I said.

"Call me, Dahlia, please," she said. I nodded, although I knew I never would.

When they left to go inside, I peered through the doors again and noticed two buses, the kind used by tour group companies, pulling up in front of the school. The doors opened, and out spilled large groups of people. These were probably the groups to whom all those extra tickets had gone. The first person off the first bus was a brown-haired man in a suit and tie smiling genially as he helped the others off, holding out his hand to the women trying to navigate their way down the steps in heels and skirts. Something about him reminded me of my dad: the ease with which he carried himself, his polite and gentlemanly manner. There was something else about him too that seemed familiar, something I couldn't quite pinpoint.

A crackling voice through a loudspeaker announced that the performance would start in a few minutes and urged everyone to take their seats. In the crowd, I couldn't find my family. I hurried to see if the girls needed help with any last-minute ushering. None of the group members had seats and had to stand in the aisles. As the lights started to dim, I looked into the auditorium. I was filled with pride at what I had helped organize, at the rows of smiling people clutching their programs. I saw Renuka and her parents with Mr. Jeremy. My eyes scanned the room for my father and Sangita. It was not like my father to be late.

Just then I caught sight of him rushing in, the edge of his jacket almost getting caught on the door handle, Sangita trailing behind him.

I gasped when I saw my mother with him, wearing the same pale yellow outfit she had on the last time I had seen her dressed up, on the night Mr. Jeremy had come over. She looked around nervously, holding my father's arm with one hand, a handkerchief pressed into her other. Once settled in her seat, my mother gazed around the room and caught my eye. She smiled warmly and gave me a small wave. My heart soared, and a lump caught in my throat. I almost cried.

Amina appeared onstage holding a small stack of index cards. The bright overhead lights reflected off her glasses, causing her to shift her position in front of the microphone. She stared out at all those expectant faces looking back at her and turned a slight shade of white. She cleared her throat, quickly gathered herself, and consulted her cards.

"Good evening, ladies and gentlemen," she said, her voice trembling a little. "Thank you all so much for making it here tonight."

She straightened her back, took a deep breath that could be heard through the microphone, and then, in a flash, lost her nervousness. Now speaking confidently, and in her very precise and impeccable way, Amina spent a few minutes talking about the outreach programs that Food4Life was contributing to in small ways.

"It truly is about so much more than food," she said, her voice resonant in the silent auditorium. "It's about empowering women so they can look after themselves and their families, giving them what they need not just to survive but to flourish."

She thanked the members of the Valley Crest Youth Orchestra for donating their time and talent. And then she turned over her last index card.

"And I'd like to give a special shout-out to the rest of my group. None of this would have been possible without the dedication of Catherine Cho, Justine Piva, and Patrick Ford. And to Shalini Agarwal, I'd just like to add one thing." She turned to look at me as I leaned against a wall. "You were the last to join but jumped right in. You understand the problems facing women in the developing world. And in you I'd like to think I've found a good friend, and a sister."

I couldn't stop the tears now. I felt so overwhelmed. First, seeing my mother out of the house and at a place that wasn't the doctor's office. And then being publicly acknowledged by a girl I admired. My parents looked over at me with pride, Sangita waving and bouncing up and down in her seat like the young girl she was. I found the tissue I always kept tucked beneath my watch strap, pulled it out, and blew my nose.

Amina continued.

"Now please, sit back and relax. You're in for a real treat."

Amina moved offstage as the red-velvet curtains behind her parted. The musicians were in their places, all dressed in black. My eyes skimmed around them till they found Toby and happily settled there. He was focused on the conductor and his baton.

There was a big group piece, rousing and jubilant, and a few solos. Then Toby stepped forward to play a duet with Dina, the pianist. It was Pergolesi's Concerto in G Major. They played in perfect sync, a connection between them where they could hear each other's music while playing along to their own.

I wanted to be that girl at the piano. Just for one night I wanted her skinny arms and nimble hands and intense gaze. I wanted to be that close to Toby, just the two of us united by a dark auditorium and the bright glare of a spotlight, enjoying the intimacy of a gorgeous musical duet.

At the end of the concert there was a standing ovation, an encore. The evening had been a startling success.

Later, I found my parents in the front hall. I felt relaxed and relieved, and my mother came up to me and hugged me.

"Very nice concert," my mother said as if I had been up on that stage. "Very nice school." It occurred to me then that, seven months into our being here, she had never seen my school from the inside.

"I'm so happy you came, Ma," I replied.

Behind her, I saw Toby emerging from the auditorium holding his case. He was searching for someone. He smiled in another direction and walked up to the man whom I had seen earlier helping people off that private bus. It must be Toby's dad. They had the same wavy hair, the same cheerful demeanor. They embraced and started to head out of the building.

I don't know what I was thinking, or if I was thinking anything at all. I told my parents I'd be right back and then sprinted over to the exit. I stood there and pretended I was waiting for someone. Toby would *have* to pass me to leave here. He would have to speak to me.

Toby and his father approached, and Toby slowed down when he saw me.

"Hey," Toby said. "Good night."

"Oh, yes, good night," I replied, stepping aside. "Bye."

"No, I mean it *was* a good night," he clarified. "Wasn't it?"

"Oh, of course it was," I said, feeling stupid now. "You played very well."

"This is my dad," he said, motioning to his father. They had virtually the same face. "Dad, this is one of the organizers. Shalini."

"I'm very pleased to meet you," his father said, extending a hand. "You kids put on quite a show tonight. Congratulations."

"I like your outfit," Toby said.

"It's Indian," I replied. It seemed that everything I was saying was either stupid or self-evident.

"I'm heading off with some of my friends to check out a new band," he said. "The lead has kind of a Ziggy

Marley vibe. You'd think that after playing in a concert the last thing I'd want to do is hear more music. But nooooooo."

Was he going to ask me to join them? Please, please, ask me, I thought. I would never be able to go, but I just wanted to be asked.

"I better get going," he said. "The guys are waiting for me outside."

I moved away, feeling suddenly squat and uninteresting.

"See ya around," he said, leaving with his father.

Twenty

BY THE TIME WE GOT HOME, I was exhausted. I changed, pulled my hair back into a ponytail, and came downstairs. I passed my mother on the steps; she was headed up, holding a cup of hot tea, telling me how tired she was. I wanted to sit and talk to her on the couch downstairs, the way we had done in our first few days here, before the depression set in. But I didn't want to push it. She'd had enough excitement for one night.

I sat down to write a long email to Vikram, telling him how successful the night had been, how people had loved the concert, and how much money we had made. I filled my letter with an abundance of details—what I wore, what filling was in the *samosas* we sold—and as I wrote, I wondered if I was doing that because I felt guilty that the only person I was really thinking about was Toby.

Just as I was signing off, Amina called. She sounded tired too, but happy.

"It was Toby's dad who bought those remaining tickets," she said. "He brought over a bunch of people who work for him."

"Yes, I figured it was something like that," I said.

"He does a lot for charity," she continued. "Made a big chunk of money in medical equipment. They're pretty wealthy."

"Oh," I said. That fact didn't impress me.

"Does he have a girlfriend?" I blurted out.

Amina giggled.

"I've never seen him with any one girl," she said. "But he's really popular with everyone. You know, he's smart, funny, athletic, plays the flute like a friggin' genius. And he's hot. Why?" she said.

"Oh, nothing. Just curious."

"Are you into him?" she asked. "Oh my God, you *are* into him!" she exclaimed as if she had just stumbled across a great, secret treasure.

"Don't be silly Amina," I said, a little embarrassed. I told her I wanted to go to bed. I knew she was teasing me. But I also knew she had every right to. Toby was cute, kind, rich, popular. And I was, in comparison, a nobody. A nobody with a fiancé.

I went to bed but couldn't sleep. Sangita was fast asleep, and the rest of the house was quiet. I stared out the window and into the room of a house across the street, where a large-screen TV played a late-night movie in a darkened room, its images flickering against white walls. I got out of bed again, paced around the room, found a book, and got back in. I flicked through the pages but couldn't bring myself to focus on anything.

This whole thing was making me sick.

I hated what I was feeling for Toby and what as a consequence I was *not* feeling for Vikram. I hated that when I was in that auditorium. I really wanted to be with Toby, a boy I could never have, while the boy I should want was thousands of miles away, missing me, waiting for me to return.

I hated what had become of my sane, planned, prepared life.

On Friday afternoon a week after the concert, my father called on his way home from work.

"I have a flat tire," he said. "I need to wait for AAA to put on the spare. We must get the tire fixed tomorrow. Maybe before we go grocery shopping." I told my father yes, no problem; after all these months here, he still relied on Sangita and me to help with the weekly food purchases. On his own, he would walk into a supermarket and not know where to even begin. It had been my mother's role, and now my younger sister and I had assumed it.

The next morning we went to our local dealership to get the spare replaced. After we dropped off the car we walked across the street to the Apple store in the mall, where my father wanted to go and look at the iPad. He was talking to a sales associate while Sangita and I went to play with the multicolored iPods, the ones that so many of our schoolmates had.

"They're neat, huh?" I heard someone behind me say. I whipped around. It couldn't be. But there he was, in front of me. Toby. It was the first time I'd seen him outside of school, so it took my brain a second to recognize him.

"Oh, hi," I said, stunned. "My dad had a flat tire. Our tire is being repaired, across the street." I was rambling. He hadn't asked me a single thing; and here I was, giving him a blow-by-blow account of my morning activities.

"Okay then," he said, smiling impishly. He smelled delicious, and a tiny tuft of hair was stuck to his cheek. His top button was only halfway through its hole.

"What about you?" I asked, trying to sound relaxed. "What brings you to these parts?" God, that sounded awful. I wanted to smack my forehead.

"It's the Apple store," he drawled. "My favorite hangout. My dad's too, although he'd never admit it."

"Cool," I said. I cringed. It was not an expression that exactly rolled off my tongue.

Sangita, who had been standing quietly next to me, spoke up.

"Hello," she said, extending her hand. "I'm Sangita. Shalini's younger sister. Who are you?"

"My name's Toby. Your sister and I met during the concert, you know, the charity thing. She helped organize it."

"Oh yes," Sangita said now, peering at him. "I remember you. On the flute." I looked over at her, puzzled that she would have noticed.

"It was a *long* concert," she said, rolling her eyes. "When you're staring at a group of people for that long, you'll remember them."

Toby and I both laughed. Sangita went back to checking out iPods.

"So, you got any other fund-raisers coming up?" he asked me.

"No," I replied. "That was our biggest one. Thought we'd end the year on a good note.

"How long have you been playing?" I said. It was something I'd always wanted to know but never had the chance to ask. Up until now our interactions had been all business, very short and to the point. Now here we were, at an Apple store, a place that I wouldn't have ordinarily come to. It was like destiny had intervened to puncture my father's tire. I was sure Toby had things to do, gadgets to play with. But for these few minutes, I had his attention.

"My dad bought me a little flute when I was four. We were walking past a music store, and I pointed at it in the window and said, 'I want that.' He didn't buy it for me right away 'cuz if every parent got every four-year-old everything they asked for, the world would be a pretty crazy place. But eventually he gave in. I started lessons when I was five. My parents tell me I even slept with my flute back then. They say it was my best friend." People milled around us, but I didn't care. I was completely focused on Toby.

"Krishna plays it," I said.

"Who?" he asked.

"Krishna. He's a Hindu god. He has blue skin. It's his magical instrument. All the maidens of the village come running when they hear him."

"Lucky dude," said Toby.

His father approached us, said a polite hello, held up his purchase.

"Got what I needed," he said to his son. "Let's head out."

Toby said a quick good-bye and left with his father. Sangita and I stared after him. "*Didi*, he's *so* cute," she said.

"*Shhh*," I whispered. Then she and I collapsed in a fit of giggles.

On Monday, at the end of the school day, I was waiting for Sangita so we could walk home together. I saw Toby in the parking lot throwing his stuff into the backseat of his gray Prius and getting into the driver's seat. He looked up and saw me standing on the steps, and came running back toward the school until he was within shouting distance.

"Need a ride somewhere?" he yelled out.

"No thank you," I shouted back. "I'm waiting for my sister."

I had a huge smile on my face all the way home.

I was still in a good mood when Vikram called that evening. He had been prepping for exams and helping his parents take care of a sick relative, so had been preoccupied lately.

"We haven't talked in almost a week," he said to me. It could have been longer. I felt so distant from him. "How are you?"

"Very good. So busy. Amina wants to start talking about fund-raisers for the fall. And remember that girl who used to be horrible to me? Sasha? She asked me to look over her English paper. So weird. It's like after all this time of being invisible, people finally see me."

"You sound happy, Shalu," he said. "It's nice."

I sighed deeply. He was such a tremendously kind boy, and I loved that so much about him.

"I am happy, I guess," I said. I fingered my ruby ring. "You were right. You told me it would just take a little time to settle in. But now that I have a few friends and a routine, my life here is not so bad."

"Well, don't forget about me," Vikram said, laughing.

"Never," I said. But when I hung up, I couldn't shake the discomfort that had descended on me.

Two days later Charlie asked me if I would meet him in the library for a refresher session, just to nail some algebra problems before finals. After Charlie left I was packing my things to leave. Toby walked in, a backpack slung over his shoulder. I was thrilled to see him but didn't show it.

He sidled up to me.

"Hey," he whispered. "What's going on?" I pointed to the door, indicating I was about to leave.

"I'm just getting started," he whispered. "But I'll walk you out." He dropped his backpack on the table and followed me.

Once we were outside he said, "I Googled Krishna."

I laughed. "I didn't realize that Krishna could be Googled," I said.

"Oh yeah. There were twelve-and-a-half million pages on him. Some nice pictures too. His flute is sweet."

"Yours is sweet too," I said, realizing that the words sounded awkward.

"Where you headed?" he asked.

"Home," I said. "I live a few blocks away."

He paused for a second, looking at me, a thin frown on his forehead.

"You know, I think I need to stretch my legs before I hit the books," he said. "I'll walk you."

Twenty-one

EVEN THOUGH I WAS ENGAGED, I'd never been out alone with my fiancé. Vikram and I had yet to go to dinner or to the movies by ourselves, where, if we had been of a different culture and from different families, we might have held hands in the back row.

I reckon that even if I wasn't engaged, I still wouldn't be allowed to date. At my school in India, it wasn't something that was done, not like here, where I'd hear a girl sobbing in the bathroom, confiding to a friend about a guy she'd made out with who no longer looked at her. Sometimes I'd see kids walk out of the school holding hands, kissing as they parted at the curb. In the smallest way, I envied the freedom in which they lived.

So to me, this walk home with Toby was momentous

and profoundly romantic. It was a huge leap forward, a step that showed I was more immersed in this culture today than I was yesterday, more grown-up, more American. A boy—a particularly good-looking, popular, well-known boy who also happened to be a senior—had stopped what he was doing to take a short walk with me around the block . . . me, a girl who had never seen herself as either good-looking, popular, or well-known.

Strangely though, as significant as this afternoon was turning out to be, I was not in the least bit nervous. There was something about Toby, something calming and confident about how he carried himself, that was rubbing off on me.

He started telling me about his parents, his home life.

"My dad is the son of German immigrants, but my mother is from Tehran," he said. I nodded. That would explain those exotic good looks: the dark hair and fair skin.

"My parents want me and my sister to have the best of both cultures," he said. "So I speak three languages, but my Farsi kind of sucks."

I laughed. My feet kept in time with his as we walked, my head tilting down, my eyes glancing sideways at him to show him that I had been listening, had heard every word.

"Tell me about you," he said.

"I arrived from Bangalore last September," I said. "I had never left India before. I lived there with thirty-seven relatives in a big house, parts of which I am quite sure were built illegally. I missed the noise of my old home. It has been difficult for me. But it is better now. Now I like it here."

For a moment he said nothing. He simply gazed at me, those long lashes framing his eyes. He squinted to avoid the glare of the sun. A bird twittered in an overhead branch and fluttered off. A mail truck stopped across the street. But all I heard, saw, was him.

He lightly touched my shoulder.

"Good," he said. "You deserve to like it here."

I was still in a daze when I stepped into our home. My mother was sitting on the couch in the den, knitting. I was so pleased to see her with her needles and a ball of yarn. She used to knit all the time in India, but I hadn't even seen her knitting bag since we got here. It was like a tiny light had been turned on somewhere.

"How are you feeling, Ma?" I asked her. "Can I bring you anything?"

"Come, *beta*, sit," she said, patting the space on the couch next to her.

I sat down, and she took my hand in hers. Her palms

were surprisingly cold, but soft.

"What is troubling you?" she asked.

"Wh . . . what do you mean, Ma?" I stammered.

"I am not blind, my child," she said. "You are not the same. There is something on your mind, something that is worrying you. I have not been well; but I am still your mother; and I know you like nobody else."

I began to cry. I wanted to tell her but couldn't because I didn't know how to, and I didn't know what I was feeling. I loved Vikram. But I was attracted to Toby. I missed home. I was happy here. I no longer knew what I wanted. I no longer knew who I was. I didn't know how to say any of this to her in a way that she would understand because I didn't understand it myself.

"It's nothing, Ma, really," I said. "I'm just worried about you. That's all."

She pulled my head to her shoulder. She didn't say anything. The knitting needles and ball fell to the floor. That tiny light seemed to have gone off again.

"Come, Ma," I said. "It's time to take your medicine."

As the school year drew to a close, there seemed to be only four things occupying the minds of the high school students: prom, finals, graduation, and summer plans— and not necessarily in that order.

I really didn't concern myself with the first two. I was secretly relieved that there was no junior prom at my school, unlike at Renuka's, where she was all set to go to hers with a group of friends. But I was certain that Toby would be going; no popular and well-liked boy would stay home that night. It gnawed away at me that he was, and that he would be going with some mystery girl who wasn't me.

The whole school was prepping for finals, everyone in a flux of all-night cramming sessions and extra, last-minute tutoring. I wasn't worried about my exams, and happily stepped in to help some of my classmates who needed it. I didn't mind being known for being smart. But despite the stress around exams, there was a vaguely celebratory mood around school, a shared relief.

Amina, Justine, Patrick, and Catherine scheduled our last meeting of the semester. When we came back in September, we would all be one year higher, one year closer to college. Toby wouldn't be in this school anymore, a thought that filled me with sadness.

Since our last encounter, that precious walk to my home, I hadn't seen him around school much. He had emailed me a couple of times; but I had been one of many, just another recipient of a funny YouTube video or silly joke. He had waved to me as he was leaving the cafeteria one day just as I was entering, shouting out a "Hey!" I didn't want him to tell me "Hey." I wanted him to love me. I stupidly, insanely, illogically, wanted him to love me.

And Vikram, despite all this, loved me still. He wrote poetry in thick black ink on red cards. He mailed me a package of some of the latest Indian CDs, even though I'd told him that everything was available in America, mimicking what my father had said to my mother once.

And my mother. I didn't know what to make of my mother. She dropped in and out of our lives like a transient, some moments lucid and present, others vapid and vacant. The latest round of drugs gave her constipation, and the subsequent laxatives gave her nausea, and the nausea lead to light-headedness; and there we were, spinning round and round in a cycle of my mother's intermittent madness. In all of this, my father was the sole constant, the glue that held us all together.

Amina was spending part of the summer volunteering at an orphanage in Dhaka, close to where her father was born.

"I hope we all have a great vacation," she said, looking at us as we sat around a teak table on the school grounds. "But I'd also like you to think a little about what we could do next year that could outdo the success of the concert.

Let's come up with something really awesome that could raise a big chunk of change. Okay?"

"What are your plans?" Amina asked later, talking to me through a mouthful of egg salad sandwich after the others went off.

"Nothing much. Just hanging around at home. My sister is going to swimming camp. I thought I'd stay with my mom." I wasn't looking forward to the summer. Renuka and her parents were spending a few weeks in Europe and then she had signed up for a visual arts program. It seemed that everyone had plans but me.

"There are so many great summer camps," she said. "I heard about a fantastic residential math program in Canada. That's your thing, right? Or if you want to do something less academic, you could study Spanish in Costa Rica or do community service in Sicily. If I hadn't already planned on going to Bangladesh, I'd probably try something wild like that."

"My parents won't agree to me going somewhere by myself, even if it's for my studies," I said.

"There's a lot that's closer to home," she said. "Day camps. There's even something here at the school. Could be cool."

"I'll think about it," I said, knowing that I would do no such thing.

The next day as I stood by my locker, I felt a light tap on my shoulder. It was Toby. I was thrilled to see him.

"So get this," he said. "Me and my dad were driving around Culver City the other day, and we passed the Krishna temple, so I told him we just *had* to stop. We went in there. It was super-cool. A few people were sitting in the back listening to music. And it had a great vegetarian restaurant. The food was amazing. I thought of you."

I knew exactly the place he was talking about. My spirits were soaring now, not just because Toby had stopped to talk, but because, while he was with his father many miles away, he had seen something that made him think of me.

"Going away for the summer?" he asked. I was holding my satchel behind my back, swinging it slowly from one side to another, feeling it gently thump on the back of my legs.

"No," I said. "You?"

"I'm going to be a teaching assistant at the music camp here. Kinda made sense since I'm gonna major in it in the fall. I'm going to Colburn. My first pick was Juilliard, but I didn't get in." He paused for a second. "It's not so bad; I'll be close to home." I silently cheered.

"Anyway, I just want finals to be done with. But you

should sign up for summer camp here," he said. "They got everything: math, literature, drama. Field trips too. Like regular school but with less people, and everyone is totally relaxed."

"I hadn't thought of it," I said.

"Look into it. It'll be fun," he said.

I was trying to hide my elation at being asked to do something with him, a way to see him every day. He turned to leave.

"Oh, Toby, wait," I said.

He turned back around.

"Are you going to prom?" I blurted. The idea of him going with another girl had haunted me more than I thought. I regretted the question as soon as it left my mouth. It was none of my business.

"Yeah, I'm going," he said. "A bunch of us are."

"Oh," I said.

"Why?" he asked. "What's the deal?"

"Oh, no, no deal," I said. I looked down at the floor, staring at the shiny tile beneath my feet. A couple kissed briefly on the lips three lockers down.

"Okay, gotta run," he said. He walked a few paces down, stopped, and turned around again.

"It's just me and a bunch of friends. No biggie," he said. "Really."

It was as if he was trying to reassure me, even though I had no right to feel insecure. It was humiliating.

Far easier for me were finals, which were a breeze. I whizzed through math and finished my English paper twenty minutes before everyone else. I could already see the As I'd get in Social Studies and Science. My rigorous education in India had served me well here. Vikram called me after every exam to see how I'd done, and before each to wish me luck. He seemed to love me as much as he did before I'd left India, maybe even more.

My father needed very little convincing that summer camp would be a good option for me. He had lots of work to get through. And he didn't want me sacrificing my summer on behalf of my mother.

"We'll manage," he said. "She'll manage."

Twenty-two

THE FIRST DAY of summer camp was like being in a completely different place. The usually crowded halls were thinned out. Everything was quieter. I liked how it felt.

I had chosen to focus on math. I had a new teacher, Mrs. Brockwell, who had a knack for making precalculus fun. It was intense: two-hour sessions followed by a break and then a couple of hours more. But it was an immersion program, designed for AP students. I fit right in. It also felt strange not having Sangita accompany me to school each day, as she did during the regular semester. She had signed up for a swim-and-sports camp and was on a completely different schedule.

On that first day I saw Toby at lunchtime, standing in

front of a vending machine. I approached him from behind.

"Hey," he said, jumping back a little bit. "You startled me."

"Sorry," I said. "I wanted to say hello. Thank you for encouraging me to do this. I'm really enjoying it so far."

"Cool," he said.

"How was graduation?" I asked. He must have looked irresistible in that navy blue robe, a scroll in his long-fingered hand. I had vowed not to ask him about prom.

"Felt great," he said. "My folks were proud, which doesn't suck."

"And how are your classes going?" I asked. He was so easy to talk to.

"Good so far, I think," he replied. "We're focusing on vibrato, which doesn't really work with Baroque. But hopefully there'll be time for me to try an awesome Debussy piece."

"Oh," I said. My face was a blank.

He laughed.

"Sorry, I must have sounded like a total douche," he said.

He was holding a bag of pretzels from the machine and now opened it and offered some to me. I reached in and pulled out a few.

We started walking out together. It seemed as if

neither of us had anywhere to be.

"Is that lunch for you?" I asked. "A bag of pretzels?"

He tossed a couple more pretzels into his mouth, crunched loudly, and shrugged.

"Do you like Indian food?" I asked.

The two of us sat on a wooden bench on the school grounds, the rice and vegetables I had prepared the night before laid out, the faint smell of cloves and cinnamon lingering in the air between us. Toby and I shared a meal, and I wanted it to never end.

A week into summer camp as I walked home, I realized that if Toby had preoccupied me before the start of the session, now there was no getting away from him. I harbored a longing—an unexpected, illogical longing—for a boy who was not my fiancé. It was stupid, senseless, so out of character for me. But no matter what I told myself, I couldn't get over my feelings for the dark-haired flute player I was just starting to know.

It was the middle of the afternoon. It was perfect weather, so reminiscent of Bangalore, with just a touch of humidity in the air and the stillness broken by a slight, occasional breeze. I could hear the jingling music from an ice cream truck that had pulled up at a park down the block. A long-haired young boy with his cap on backward whizzed by on his skateboard. Across the street, a man was cleaning his garage, stacking cardboard boxes and filling big black plastic bags with trash. My heart felt strangely calm, my head clear. I looked at my ring again. I felt ripped in two. I had fallen for Toby, but right now there was nothing I could do about it.

On the approach to my house, my feet suddenly stopped moving. I stared out at the patch of grass outside. A woman wearing a wide-brimmed hat and holding a small shovel hacked away at the dirt. A row of perennials had been gouged out of the ground.

If it wasn't for the nightgown, I wouldn't have recognized her.

"Ma! What are you doing?" I shouted, running now.

She looked up and raised her hand above her eyes to shield them from the sun.

"I'm gardening," she said. "I was just watching it on TV. Remember that small area behind Dada's house where I used to grow onions and basil? I used to love going out there, to see what had sprouted." She looked back down again at the dirt, her eyes vacant.

"Your sister is swimming," she said, continuing to dig. "Your papa is working. You are studying. Everyone is busy doing something. So I thought, 'Okay, I will garden!'" She started to laugh, a forced, contrived laugh.

"Ma, please come inside. Papa must be on his way home with Sangita."

She calmly went on plunging the shovel into the ground.

"Please, Ma, you shouldn't be out in your night-clothes."

"Like anyone will notice!" she said loudly, her eyes narrowing. "They are all in their own world. I can be here wearing nothing, and nobody would care."

She was trembling. I dropped my satchel and put my arms around her. Just then my father's car pulled up. Sangita was sitting next to him in the front, her wet hair clinging to her head. They both looked through the windshield, astonished.

My father leaped from the car.

"What is happening here?" he asked, his eyes wide behind his glasses. "Asha, what is this? What are you doing? What happened to our flowers?"

My mother stared at him from under the hat.

"You want your flowers? Here! Here are your flowers!" she shouted, picking them up from the ground and tossing them at him.

"Come, Asha, let's go inside," my father said, more calmly now.

My mother stood firm for a second, but my father put

his arm around her shoulders. I stood on the other side, and she crumpled between us. We escorted her into the house. The dirt fell off her nightgown onto the carpet. My father reached over and pulled off her hat.

He led her into the den and eased her gently onto the couch, telling Sangita to fetch her some water. My mother threw her head back onto the cushion and closed her eyes.

"Why did you bring me here?" she said, sobbing now. She opened her eyes and looked straight at my father. "You never even asked me. You just decided; and you brought me, all of us. I miss home so much." She was crying hard now. My father's face was a blank. He looked over at me.

"Bring her medicine," my father instructed me.

I ran upstairs, leaping over two steps at a time, and into my parents' bedroom. The orange bottles weren't in their usual spot on the dressing table. I went into the bathroom. The bottles had been emptied and were lying in the trash atop a pile of used Kleenex. I happened to glance into the toilet bowl. At the bottom of the water, in a neat little pile, were handfuls of partially dissolved pills. I took the empty bottles downstairs to my father. He looked at them and then back at my mother, who was quiet again, her cheeks stained with tears. Then he went to the phone and called Dr. Gupta. I followed him, while Sangita stayed with our mother. He spoke quickly to the doctor, told her what had happened, nodded at what she was saying, hung up.

"It is normal," he said, frowning. "The doctor says that this talking she has been doing with the other women, this sharing of feelings, has stirred some things in her. She says it is not a bad thing, what has happened. She needed to speak her mind, show us her true feelings. It is better than saying nothing."

My father and I went to pick up a new batch of pills, which Dr. Gupta suggested we put in my mother's food. She said that my mother should not be left alone, at least not until the pills kicked in. Sangita, my father, and I came up with a timetable.

Late one night I came downstairs to get some milk. My father was sitting on the couch listening to music, his head resting in his hand.

"Papa?" I said gently.

Startled, he opened his eyes.

"What's the matter, Papa? Why aren't you in bed?"

"I have some decisions to make," he said, rubbing his eyes now.

I sat down on the ottoman next to him.

"Tell me, Papa," I said.

He reached out and touched my hand.

"You have always been such a good girl, a good daughter," he said, sitting forward. Then he leaned back in his seat again.

"Mr. Jeremy has been talking to me about extending my contract."

I sat upright.

"But one year is not even up yet!" I said, stating the obvious.

"I know," my father said quietly. "But what has surprised me is not that he has asked, but that I have been considering it," he said quietly. "I am enjoying it here, my life, my work. I feel useful, valued. Despite all the unhappiness that has been caused by our move, I want to stay. I must be crazy."

"Sangita and I are not unhappy," I said. "In fact, I think Sangita is happier than I have ever seen her. She thinks she's the next Michael Phelps." I laughed weakly.

"And what about you and your Vikram?" Papa asked. "You are miserable without him."

I wanted to correct him but didn't. I *was* once miserable without him. But not anymore. I had filled my life with other things.

"Don't worry about Vikram and me," I said. "We have

all our lives to be together." I paused. "What about Dada? You promised Dada you would go back in two years."

"I will handle Dada," my father said with surprising determination. "I am a grown man, after all."

"So it's just Ma then," I said quietly.

"Yes, it's just her."

Twenty-three

I TOLD TOBY ABOUT MY MOTHER: the depression, the doctor, everything. After I finished recounting the gardening incident, he nodded thoughtfully.

"So she had a complete meltdown," he said. "Maybe it's not such a bad thing."

"Really?" I asked.

"Sure." He shrugged. "She probably needed to freak out a little. Beats lying in bed all day doped up on drugs."

We were sitting on a mat having lunch on the school lawn. He reached into a brown bag and pulled out a small baguette packed with slices of turkey and tomatoes. I unfolded the plastic wrap around my cheese-and-chutney sandwich and took a bite.

Toby reached over with a napkin and wiped off a

smear of the green mint sauce from near my lip.

"Thanks," I said, feeling a little awkward.

He stared at me.

"You're cute," he said.

I looked down.

"I'm not. You don't have to say that," I replied. In my family, vanity was discouraged. I had always believed that the only reason I had landed a catch like Vikram was because our fathers had decreed it.

"You are. You're just naturally cute. There's nothing phony about you."

I was overcome with embarrassment now. I didn't know how to respond. If it had come from anybody else, I would have sworn I was being made fun of.

"You're a great girl, Shalini," he said, putting down his sandwich and picking up a bottle of water. He was looking straight into my eyes with a directness that took me by surprise. "You care about people. You are who you are. I think that's pretty hot."

I stopped breathing. I didn't know where this was going, why he was telling me this. But I loved it. Deep down inside, way beneath the dim view I held of myself, I loved hearing his words. I could tell he meant what he said. As wrong as I knew it was—that I was in love with this gorgeous boy with the dark wavy hair and the silver flute pressed to his lips—I loved what he was saying. I stared at my ruby ring and denied the guilt that was forming around my heart.

At home, my mother looked a little better. She had showered, and there was a pinkness to her cheeks. She was mopping, and humming. I wondered how long she would be like this.

"Vikram called this morning after you left for school," she said. She stood upright, leaning against the handle of the mop. "Is everything okay between you two?" she asked.

"Of course, Ma," I said. "Why wouldn't it be?"

That night, after everyone had gone to bed, I called him back. He was done with college for the summer and planned to do some traveling with his parents. He was hosting a party with some friends. There was a new dance club in town he wanted to check out. He sounded busy and happy. Someone had sent him a silly video.

"Oh, I know that one," I said excitedly. "Toby sent it to me."

He paused.

"Who?" he asked.

"Oh, nobody. Nothing." I was flustered. "Toby. He's just a guy at my school. He plays the flute."

"You haven't mentioned him before. Is he a new friend?"

"Kind of," I said. "I met him during the big concert."

"Oh," said Vikram. "It's just that you told me everything about that concert, and you didn't mention him."

There was silence. My mind raced. What was I hiding? The truth was, we *were* just friends. We sat on springy fresh grass and ate sandwiches, and sometimes he played the flute for me. He told me I was cute, and I couldn't stop thinking about him. I didn't tell Vikram anything because I didn't know what to tell him.

"Vikram, please, it is nothing. He's just a guy. Let's talk about something else. How's your mother?"

Right before the last week of summer camp, there was an all-school outing, a hike along a popular trail in Malibu. I had never been hiking before. My father signed the permission slip, although he felt the need to point out that he didn't see what hiking had to do with mathematics and was he paying for me to learn or was he paying for me to be out in nature?

I packed a bag with bottled water, bags of trail mix, and fresh red apples. I imagined myself walking alongside Toby as our feet crunched against the leaves on the ground, how he would point out medicinal plants and edible berries on the way. My brand-new bright white sneakers, bought just for this, pinched my toes. I couldn't wait.

My father dropped me off at the meeting place. Everyone was already there, Toby standing tall among them. He waved when he saw me. The group leader handed out maps and brochures. We walked half a mile up a gravelly incline, me pulling at weeds and grabbing on to rocks to avoid falling over backward. It was more strenuous than I had thought it was going to be. Toby grabbed my hand at one point, and even after I steadied myself, he clung onto it. I wiggled my fingers and he released my hand, his eyes fleetingly meeting mine.

After a couple of hours I was relieved to be told we were taking a break for lunch. We found a resting spot on an embankment that sloped down gently to a creek. It was remarkably quiet, a stillness settling on the vastness of the land around us. Everyone got comfortable, unzipping backpacks and opening Tupperware containers. I placed my bag between my legs and reached in for my lunch. Toby, next to me, held up a McDonald's bag.

"Drive-through," he said. "Yup, first class all the way."

I giggled and stretched out my legs, forgetting that my backpack was resting between them. The bag went tumbling down the embankment toward the creek. I squealed and put my hand over my mouth. Toby leaped up and went racing down after it. Everyone turned to look, laughing and pointing. By the time Toby reached the creek, the bag was already steeped in the stagnant waters, the apples bobbing around on top, the bags of raisins and walnuts soaked through, my plastic water bottle floating off down the creek. He picked up my drenched backpack, shook it off, and came clambering back up.

"Sorry I couldn't get to it fast enough," he said, handing it back to me.

"Thank you," I said, taking it from him. We looked at each other and both burst into laughter. I laughed so hard that I didn't care about the sun glinting off my braces or the guttural sound I made when I took a breath between chortles, the one that my cousins always teased me about. I couldn't remember the last time I had laughed like that.

Toby sat back down next to me and teasingly rubbed his shoulder against mine.

"Goofball," he said. From his McDonald's bag, he pulled out a small fries, now cold and droopy, and handed it to me. Some of the other people in our group came up to me, each handing me something from their lunch: yogurt, chips, a granola bar, sweet orange wedges. I was moved by their generosity, and noticed that my shoulder was still touching Toby's, neither one of us moving away.

Full and rested, we began hiking again. Our leader

said we would make a loop toward the end of the trail, near a waterfall, and head back. We splintered off into smaller groups, a few couples here and there, some people walking on their own. Toby and I somehow kept in step with each other; occasionally we were joined by some of the others, sometimes it was just the two of us. He was slowing down so I could keep up with him. Over some especially tough terrain—tough for me, anyway—he offered to hold my bag.

The waterfall was set in a forestlike grove: leafy, verdant, and green. It was shaded and tranquil, a wonderful respite from the sun-exposed trail we had just been on. The waters fell into a dark pool, creating calm ripples. Some kids had come prepared and stripped down to their bathing suits for a quick swim. I sat on the edge of the cool water and watched, marveling at the natural beauty of the place. Toby eased down onto a spot next to me and picked up a dry twig. He broke it into tiny pieces and tossed them into the water.

"I was eight the first time I came here," he said, watching his friends jump from a tree into the water. "My dad brought me. I thought it was a magical grotto or something. I couldn't believe such a mysterious place existed almost in our backyard."

"It is something," I said. "I've never seen anything like it."

He was staring at me. I looked away to avoid his gaze. I was barely breathing. He felt so close, so touchable. The air between us felt heavy, unmoving.

"Come here," he said. "I want to show you something."

He gave me his hand. I grabbed it, and he helped me up. We walked through tall pine and cedar trees to the far end of the waterfall, away from the crowd. Down another short, shadowy trail we ran into the remnants of a small stone building, its surface badly eroded, pockmarked with tiny crevices. There was no ceiling, just three broken walls and large holes where windows might once have been.

"What is this place?" I asked.

"I don't really know for sure," he said. "But I had lots of theories about it. When I first saw it as a little kid, I pretended I was an adventurer sent here to find a buried treasure. I used to pick up a branch and sword fight nobody. It was pretty sad."

I imagined him at eight, a little boy clutching his father's hand, swept up by this fantastical, exotic place. My heart warmed.

"But my dad told me to knock it off. It was time to go home and practice the flute."

We both laughed.

"It'd be cool to go back in time, huh?" he said.

I closed my eyes for a second and thought of my house in Bangalore, its patios curtained with clothes hung out to dry; my grandma scolding the vegetable man for trying to off-load his wilted coriander on her; Vikram and me playing cards under a slowly whirring fan, our feet barely touching under the table. Those images used to be crystal clear, precise. But today they were faded and remote, like scenes from a movie I had seen long ago, scenes from someone else's life.

Yes, sometimes I did wish to go back in time. But right now, today, I didn't want to be anywhere else than where I was.

"We'd better go," I said to Toby, who was rubbing his hand over one of the stone bricks. He nodded and let his hand drop. He followed me, walking so close behind me I could feel his breath on my neck.

"Wait," he suddenly whispered.

I spun around.

"What?" I said. I thought that maybe he had seen a wild animal. We were up by a hefty oak tree now. A bird landed on a branch overhead, then flew off again. Toby was right up against me, so close that I could see the stubble on his chin. I was frozen, mesmerized. Before I knew what was happening, could even try to stop it, he had encircled my waist with one arm, his other arm pressed up against the tree. He bent down, and his lips touched mine, brushing against them gently. His body was strong and warm. My heart felt as if it was going to catapult out of my chest. I didn't know what to do with my hands, so I let them hang limply by my sides.

So this was what a kiss felt like. I was a sixteen-year-old girl engaged to a boy for thirteen of those years; and this, here and now, in this shady forest, was my first kiss. It was soft and beautiful, and I wanted it to never end.

I pulled back, looked down, felt dizzy.

"What's wrong?" he asked, still whispering. His forehead was touching mine now. I felt sinfully close to him.

"I'm so sorry, Toby," I said, tears gathering in my eyes.

He stepped back from me.

"What's going on?" he asked. "Did I get the vibe wrong? I thought you wanted me to kiss you."

"I did. I do," I said. I scratched my palms. "You have no idea how much I like you. I think about you all the time. You're the only reason I signed up for summer camp. I just wanted to see you every day."

His shoulders relaxed a little.

"So what then?" he asked, his voice softer now.

I held up my hand with the ring on it.

"It's this," I said.

Twenty-four

ALL THE WAY BACK DOWN the trail to the entrance to the park, Toby and I barely spoke to each other. He didn't offer to carry my backpack and walked a few steps ahead of me, one hand shoved into his jeans pocket.

My father was already waiting for me, reading the paper as he sat behind the wheel. I said a quick good-bye to the group. I looked at Toby and waved weakly, pathetically. His hand was still in his pocket. He bit his bottom lip and nodded, expressionless.

At home, all I wanted to do was shower and go to bed. The hike had left me dirty and exhausted, my conversation with Toby depleting me. My father had been in a cheerful mood all the way home, actually whistling. I had never heard my father whistle before. My mother was probably still feeling okay.

All I could think about was the look on Toby's face when I had told him about Vikram as we stood in that cool, quiet, green grotto. He had raised his eyebrows a few times, but otherwise his face had been cold, unmoving. He didn't say anything for a long time. He let me tell my story. Halfway through, I'd begun hearing it through his ears, and I'd begun seeing myself the way he most likely saw me: a downtrodden girl whose parents had made every major decision for her, whose very future was decided on her third birthday. I'd felt like a freak.

"Engaged at three, huh?" he had said. "Unbelievable."

"Are you mad?" I'd asked nervously.

"Nah, I'm not pissed," he'd said. "We were just messing around, right? It's cool that you're engaged. Really. Look, let's head back. The others will be waiting for us."

"Toby, please." I had been crying. I'd wanted him to be upset, to show some feelings. I'd hated how he was freezing me out like this.

"I didn't tell you because I was embarrassed," I had said through tears. "I thought I just had a little crush on you, something that would go away. I figured you would never feel that way about me."

But he had simply turned around and walked back to the group, leaving me following in his wake.

Showered and in bed, I looked through my diary, chewing a pen. I had texted Toby four times and got no response. Now I was trying to come up with the right word for what I was feeling. I had filled countless pages in my book of firsts; and, looking back through them now, I was struck by how silly some of the firsts were, as if vitamin water was going to be something I would always remember. Sangita, reading in the bed next to mine, turned to look at me.

"What is the matter, *didi*?" she asked, the light from the bedside lamp reflecting off her tiny glasses. "You are upset tonight. Did something happen on your hike today?"

She was still a child, innocent. She still sometimes crawled into bed with my parents at night. I was her smart and sensible older sister, the girl who never made mistakes, the one who always did the right thing.

"Come on, *didi*, you can tell me," she said, putting down her book. "You know you can tell me anything."

"Really, Sangita, it's nothing," I said. "I'm just missing Vikram. I'm thinking about him a lot."

I couldn't tell her the truth, that it wasn't Vikram I

was missing but Toby. I couldn't shatter the illusion she had of me of being the perfectly behaved older sister.

I closed my eyes, and a stray tear rolled down my right cheek, landing on the lace frill of my nightgown. I opened my eyes again, went to a blank page in my diary, and wrote the word I had been seeking: "Heartbroken."

Sangita took off her glasses, laid them down carefully on the bedside table, and snuggled under the covers.

"Don't worry, *didi*," she said. "He will always be yours."

The next day I was still in a funk, unable to rouse myself from it. I kept hoping to hear from Toby; but there was nothing, not even those silly, funny, pointless videos. When the household was quiet, I considered calling him but decided against it. How many more times could I say "Sorry"? All I could do was hope he would come around on his own. Even then, what did I think was going to happen next? I placed my fingers to my lips, recalling that brief moment yesterday when I had given in to him. I had loved how he smelled, how he tasted. I felt terrible for loving it.

At five in the evening my father told me to get dressed; we were going out for dinner.

"Why?" I asked. I couldn't fathom the thought of putting on proper clothes and brushing my hair. "I don't feel like it," I said. "Can't we order in?"

"Your mother, with God's grace, is feeling a little better today," he said. "It will be a good change for her. After all, we don't know what her mood will be tomorrow."

A couple of hours later we were circling the parking lot at Chili's. My father checked his watch anxiously, almost rear-ending a car in front of him. Finally we entered the noisy restaurant and were shown to a table by the window. We ordered lettuce wraps without the chicken, burgers without the beef, cheese quesadillas, French fries, and Cokes all around. I had a headache. I wasn't even hungry.

A window on the far wall overlooked the parking lot. Someone there caught my eye.

"Papa, I think I just saw Mr. Phil," I said. My father, sitting opposite me, turned around for a second to follow my gaze.

"What a coincidence," he said, a weird smile on his face. My father was facing the door. His eyes looked over my head. He smiled broadly now.

"What happened to your *choti*?" a voice said. I drew in a sharp intake of breath and felt the blood drain out of my face. Sangita, sitting next to my father, clapped her hands gleefully.

Vikram was standing right behind me.

I felt faint. The room was spinning. I noticed the flash of his belt buckle, the hair on his arms that peeked out from beneath the cuffs of his shirt, the smidgen of pink gum that was visible when he smiled. He looked down at me, his arms raised skyward as if he were beseeching some unseen angels, and said, "Surprise!"

Twenty-five

"I'M SHOCKED," I said to him. "I had no idea. What . . . How . . . What are you doing here?"

He was sitting next to me now. He pulled his chair close to mine. I recognized his cologne. I had bought it for him on his last birthday.

"I knew before you left that I would try and come see you here," he said. "Two years is too long to be apart. I wanted to surprise you."

"But *I* knew!" Sangita said. "Papa told Ma and me. But he made me *promise* not to say anything. It was very hard. Especially last night when you were crying for him!"

Vikram, sitting next to me now, knocked his elbow against mine and winked. His hair had been recently cut, shorn close to his head. The black thread he wore for religious reasons, that he had always worn, was wound tightly against his wrist.

I couldn't believe he was here. My mother looked at both of us, her eyes darting from Vikram to me and then back to Vikram again.

"No need to cry for him now," my father said, pushing a plate of onion rings toward us. "Your Vikram has come for you."

Mr. Phil was waiting to take Vikram to his hotel. We walked out together.

"So, you didn't answer me," he said. "What happened to your *choti*?" It was the first time we were alone since he walked into the restaurant.

"Oh, I just got tired of it," I said. "Too much upkeep."

He stared at me silently.

"You look very nice, Shalini," he said at last. "Very pretty, very grown-up. You've changed a lot."

"Thank you," I said, nervous now. He was the boy I had known for sixteen years, engaged to for thirteen. I didn't have a thing to say to him. I looked into the parking lot for Mr. Phil and was relieved when he finally rolled up with the car.

* * *

He called me two hours later at home. He was jet-lagged, unable to fall asleep.

"We have a week together," he said. "I want to see everything about your life here. We have so much to catch up on, Shalu. I've really missed you. It's so good to see you."

"It's good to see you too," I said. "But try and get some rest now. We will talk tomorrow."

I hung up, made some tea, and went out to the patio. The fairy lights my father had installed on the trees last Christmas were still up, their tiny bulbs twinkling in the dark, balmy night. I sat down on one of the padded deck chairs, put my feet up, crossed my ankles, and rested my head against the soft cushion. I heard only crickets in the bushes, a sports broadcast from somewhere down the block.

I wanted to be thrilled. When I had seen Vikram, I should have jumped out of my seat, flung my arms around him, and let him twirl me around in the restaurant. That was what the old Shalu would have done. But instead, I had sat there, too stunned to move, too mystified at his decision to fly halfway across the world to see a girl who had kissed someone else, who wanted someone else. When I had seen him, I'd seen Dada and Dadi, his parents and mine, thirty-seven people steering the course of our lives. I'd seen two ruby rings picked out by his mother. I'd seen a crying three-year-old whose white party dress had been stained by pink icing and a six-year-old boy wiping her tears away.

I had seen all of that.

But I hadn't seen me. I had been "Vikram's girl" for so long, I didn't even know who I was anymore.

But a promise had been made. Where I came from, promises must be kept. Vikram was here to see me. I just *had* to love him again.

It was the last week of summer camp. I was scared to go back to regular school, but I had to. I had to talk to Toby, to make him understand. I needed him in my life again, in whatever way he chose. I just couldn't stand for him to hate me.

The heat was stultifying. I was amazed at how quickly it had turned, going from breezy and pleasant to searingly hot. At school, few people hung around outdoors. I didn't see Toby anywhere. I walked past the music room and his locker, poked my head into the lunchroom. It was all I could do to carry on with my classes.

Vikram was there when I got home in the afternoon, being given a guided tour of the house by my father. A bag lay open on the floor from which spilled gifts from

India: jars of pickled lime wrapped in twine, CDs of Bollywood music, saris, and gold jewelry.

"Call me courier," Vikram said, laughing.

The afternoon turned to evening. My mother went back to her room. The four of us had dinner together. Vikram was eager to know everything about our lives here. He commented on Sangita's deep tan, asked my father about his driver's license; then they talked about the subprime crisis as Sangita and I cleared the table. When I returned to the living room, Vikram made space for me on the couch next to him. Our hands were hidden behind a velvet cushion. He picked up my fingers and started playing with them. It should have felt comfortable and familiar. I pulled my hand away, and he turned to look at me, a slight frown on his face. When my father offered to drive him back to his hotel, I was relieved.

The following day Vikram went to have lunch with my father at his office. My father wanted to introduce his future son-in-law to his boss. I shook my head as I thought of what Mr. Jeremy, with all his modern ideas, would think of that.

At school, I saw Toby sitting on a wooden bench alone, listening to his iPod. He pulled out his earbuds when he saw me approaching. I sat down next to him.

"Hi," I said.

"Hey," he replied.

"I looked for you yesterday."

"Yeah, we were away for a couple of days. In San Francisco. Didn't get back till late last night."

"Oh, you didn't mention you were going away," I said. I realized how ironic that sounded, that I would be offended that he didn't tell me about an overnight trip with his family when I hadn't told him I was supposed to be getting married in a year.

I sat up straight and looked at him. A stray black hair was on his beige T-shirt. I reached over and pulled it off.

"I'm miserable," I said to him. "Ever since the other day. I feel like crap about everything. It's not like me to screw things up."

He turned and looked away, toward a few kids who were playing hacky sack on the grass.

"I don't want you to be miserable," he said. "Don't want you to feel like crap."

I sighed.

"He's here," I said.

Toby's head snapped back in my direction.

"Vikram. The guy. My fiancé." The words sounded awkward. "He's here. Showed up on Sunday night to surprise me."

"Good for you," Toby said.

"I don't know what to do," I said. "He's so sweet. Such a good guy. My parents love him. He loves me. I thought I loved him too. But then I came here. Everything changed. My life opened up. I met you. I heard you play the flute. I couldn't think of anything else after that." I was crying now. "I'm crazy," I said.

He wound his earbuds around his iPod and put it into a front pocket of his backpack. The bag had been sitting between us. He lifted it and put it on the ground. He moved closer to me.

"Yup," he said. "You're all kinds of crazy." He lightly put his arm around my shoulder.

I turned to him, my eyes beseeching.

"What will I do, Toby?"

He shrugged and lay his hand over mine.

Every night was spoken for. Hollywood Boulevard. Chinatown, Beverly Hills. Vikram bought a yellow Lakers hat, which he wore everywhere. He carried his father's old Nikon camera, and Sangita teased him about being the only teenager in the world who didn't have a digital camera. He joked back that he wanted to be "old school." He wanted to see everything. Some days, my mother joined us. Others, she retired early. One evening we all had dinner with Renuka and her parents. When

Vikram had gone to the restroom, Renuka told me how cute she thought he was, how hot.

"I'm kinda surprised," she said. "He just seems, you know, so nice and normal, like not the kind of guy who'd be okay with getting engaged at six."

"He's more than okay with it, Renuka," Sangita said proudly. "He *loves* my *didi*."

Renuka folded her arms in front of her, a shadow of something that looked vaguely like jealousy fleeting across her face.

She was right; there was so much about Vikram to love: whenever he said hello or good-bye to my parents, he touched their feet like the well-brought-up boy he was, and they put their hands on his head in blessing. Even though he was a guest in our city, he wanted to make sure that we were happy and comfortable.

Yet Vikram and I were never alone together, a continuation of Dada's decree despite the fact that we were thousands of miles away. I didn't mind it. Sangita continued to remind me of how happy I must be having my Vikram so near. I said nothing. I was counting the days until he would leave.

Twenty-six

VIKRAM WAS LEAVING on Friday night, catching a connecting flight in Kuala Lumpur before going on to Bangalore. He said he wanted to spend most of the day with me. It would be a year before we would see each other again.

I told him it was my last day of summer camp. I wanted to finish my classes, tie up any loose ends, and then he and I could spend the evening together before his flight.

At school, there was a picnic to celebrate the last day. I wore a new yellow top and lip gloss, my mother's dangling gold earrings. It would be my first school party.

We congregated on the green grass, freshly watered and mowed. Tables had been set up and covered with

plastic tablecloths patterned with confetti and bal-
loons. I went over and poured some Sprite into a
paper cup.

On a low wooden platform, some of the school musicians unpacked their instruments. A boy with a violin, a
girl with a cello. Toby pulled out his silver flute. He pol-
ished it while his eyes searched the crowd. They found
me, and stopped searching. I waved at him.

They were jamming—bluegrass, rock, jazz. I sat on
the grass, my knees pulled up to my chest, watching and
listening. Sasha, whom I had seen a few times around
school over the summer, asked if she could sit next to me.
She had a plate of potato salad drenched in creamy may-
onnaise. She offered me a bite and I gratefully accepted,
relishing the flavor of the fresh dill. The sun was high,
but a calming breeze had lifted away yesterday's heat. A
girl in a frayed denim skirt was tapping a tambourine
against her leg. I realized I was swaying in time to the
music. I looked around and saw familiar faces, happy
faces. Then my eyes went back to Toby, who was playing
a spirited folk number, his eyes closed, his head rhyth-
mically moving from side to side, his long fingers gliding
up and down the shiny silver instrument. I wanted to
hold his hand again, wanted those lips to caress mine. I
didn't know how this was going to work. I didn't know

what I was going to do. All I knew was that I was crazy about him.

Right then, at that moment, nothing existed beyond Toby and me.

When the music died down, he jumped off the platform and came toward me, easing himself onto the grass.

"You're so good," I said to him.

"I can teach you if you want," he said.

"I think you'll give up after one lesson," I said.

He paused, and his eyes moved all over my face, resting on my mouth.

"Maybe not," he said quietly. "I'm still here, right? I guess that's saying something." He lifted his arm and wove it behind me so it was gently touching my waist. I didn't move. His other hand was on my knee. He was wearing colored rubber bracelets. I gently fingered them.

I don't know what made me look up. There had been no noise out of the ordinary, nothing calling to me. But I glanced up and, twenty feet away, saw a boy in a yellow Lakers cap staring straight at me.

I rose and flew toward him. I thought he would turn and leave; but he stood there, rooted to the spot, staring. Behind me I heard Toby calling my name. I didn't even look back.

"Vikram!" I said, nearing him now. "What are you *doing* here?"

His eyes were wide open, the bill of his hat shadowing his face. I saw in my mind's eye what he just did: the girl he had loved all his life leaning up against another boy, touching his wrist, giggling into his neck. I saw what he had seen, and I hated myself.

He stared at me and said nothing.

"I wanted to see your school," he said. "To surprise you." He paused. "Who's that boy?" he asked. "Is that the flute boy?"

I nodded.

"You seem very friendly with him," Vikram said. His expression was stern, suspicious. "What is going on?"

"I don't know, Vikram," I said. I was crying now, again. "I need to talk to you. Let me go get my bag, then we can walk home."

I ran back toward the lawn. Toby was right where I had left him, a frown on his face.

"That was him, right?" he said. "Shit, I'm sorry."

"It's not your fault," I said. "None of it is your fault. I'm sorry. I have to go." I slung my bag over my shoulder.

"Want me to come with you?" Toby asked.

"No," I said, wiping my nose with my hand. "I made this mess. I have to fix it."

When I got back to where I had left Vikram, he was no longer there.

I ran home, hoping that was where Vikram was headed. The repercussions of what had just happened dawned on me as I sprinted down the street. I had betrayed not just Vikram, but his parents and mine, my grandparents, all my relatives, the family astrologer, the family priest; destroyed a three-decade friendship between two men; and spat on my future. I had broken the promise I had made by wearing his ring, and I had defied an oath made by two friends thirteen years ago as they sat in white wicker chairs and planned their children's lives.

I had to make this right. I didn't know how. But I just *had* to.

I tore up the driveway. The front door was unlocked. I rushed in. The house was exactly as I had left it that morning. I was enveloped in silence.

I collapsed onto the couch, put my head in my hands, and cried. He wasn't here. My first thought was that he had left without saying good-bye.

I lifted my head. On the coffee table, right in front of me, was the Nikon camera. I picked it up and looked around. Through the glass doors leading to the patio I saw him lying on a deck chair, his hands folded in his

lap, his eyes closed. His nose was red. He had been crying too.

I slid open the door. It squeaked. He opened his eyes.

I sat down in the chair next to him. I wanted to tell
him everything, but no words came out. Because no
matter what I said, I would never be able to explain it,
never be able to take away the hurt.

"I'm sorry," I said pathetically. I played with the strap
on his camera, weaving it between my fingers.

He sat up, swung his legs over the side of the chair,
and leaned forward. He took the camera from my hands.

"What's going on, Shalu?" he asked. I thought he
would sound angrier. But he sounded defeated.

I started crying again.

"I don't know," I sobbed. "I'm such a mess. I made a
mistake. Please forgive me."

"Why didn't you tell me about him?" he asked. "We
have always told each other everything."

I shook my head and looked around for a Kleenex.

"I don't know. There was never a right time. I didn't
know how much he liked me. I didn't know how much I
liked him. I was hoping it would go away. I thought it was
crazy, the feelings I had for him. All my life there was only
you. And then suddenly there was someone else."

He took off his cap and scratched his jaw. He stood

up, his jeans sagging at the waist, his shirt creased. He walked around the small patio. My eyes followed him.

"I went to your dad's office the other day," he said. "Jeremy told me he was hoping your father might stay on an extra year." His voice was serious now. This whole situation was serious. If we were in India, our families would have been here to mediate. But it was just he and I. It was up to us to figure this out.

He turned around quickly, startling me.

"I don't know how it's going to work, Shalu," he said. I knew what he was saying. I started to cry. This couldn't end. I couldn't not have him in my life. I couldn't let go of him. I wanted to take everything back, everything that had happened these past months, these past days. I wished I had never met Amina. I wished I had never met Toby. I needed Vikram. I had always needed Vikram. Inside, in so many ways, I was still three years old.

He sat down and took my hands. His fingers moved over the smooth surface of my ring.

"I was very hurt when I saw you today, with him. That was the way you used to look at me. But since I've been here, you haven't looked at me like that."

"Please, Vikram," I begged. "It's a stupid mistake. It will never happen again."

He let go of my hands, wrapped his arms around

himself. His brows were knitted together, his eyes earnest, his voice steady now.

"You are my life, my *jaan*," he said. "You always have been. I have never questioned that we would be together. Not even when you left India. Not even when you got busy with your life here. But *you* have questioned it. Since you have come here, you have questioned it. I don't blame you. But this is one thing I cannot help you with, Shalu."

As he spoke, I could only see one image; it was supposed to happen in a year: Vikram and I seated beneath a flower-covered canopy, our hands bound together by red silk thread, a priest reciting Sanskrit prayers. That had been my dream, *our* dream. I couldn't walk away from it.

"You say you love me, Shalu, and I believe you. I also know that you had no choice but to love me. We did not choose each other. I was lucky that you are the girl for me. But maybe it took your father bringing you here for you to wonder if I was the boy for you."

"But I do love you, Vikram," I said.

"Maybe one day I will know that for sure," he said. "But your life is here now. I want you to have it, whatever makes you happy. I will wait for you until you ask me not to."

My heart was physically hurting now. I was crying big, heaving sobs. Vikram leaned in again, put his fingers around mine, and gently slipped off my ring. Then he put it in my palm and enclosed my hand around it.

"Keep it," he said, using his thumbs to wipe away my tears. "But only put it on again if you are ready."

He stood up, holding me. I was shaking in his arms. He held me, my wet cheek resting against his collarbone. I touched a white button on his shirt. I didn't want him to leave.

Then I thought of Dada, of the devastation that this would have on our families, our reputations.

"I will take care of everything," Vikram said, reading my mind. I didn't ask him what he meant, only knew that he would. He had one hand on each side of my face and was stroking my cheeks. He bent down and kissed my forehead.

The front door was still open, and now Mr. Phil was standing in the doorway. Vikram let go of me, picked up his camera, and walked out.

I stood there, my body reverberating, my heart screeching. What had just happened? Had Vikram left me? Was I without him now, without him for the first time in my life? I looked around. There was nobody there, nobody to tell me I was going to be all right, no grandparents or aunts and uncles to come to my rescue. I felt bare, stripped down, helpless.

I ran upstairs. The door to my mother's room was open. She was in bed; the TV was on. A Hindi commercial for a henna shampoo was playing: an image of a young bride in red brushing her long, glossy hair. I had grown up with those images. I was supposed to be that girl.

My mother moved over, making room for me. I plopped down on the bed next to her and threw my arms around her neck, crying into her shoulder, a silk rosebud from her nightgown scratching my lip.

"Ma, I need you," I sobbed.

I felt a tremor of movement in her arms. She sat upright, gathered herself around me, and rocked me gently in her arms. She pulled my tear-soaked hair away from my face. She leaned her lips close to my ear and whispered, "Don't worry, *beta*. I'm here."

Late that night I replied to Toby's texts. Was I okay, he wanted to know. "What went down?"

I answered, "We'll talk."

The next week there was a senior-year orientation at school. We arranged to meet there afterward, on the patch of green grass where we had spent so many lunch hours during the summer.

I was already sitting on the grass as Toby walked toward me. His hands, empty of the flute case, swung casually by his sides.

"Hey," he said, crouching down. "How's it going?"

I told him what had happened. Afterward he said, "Are you okay?"

"Actually, yes," I said. He was sitting opposite me now; our knees were touching.

"It's the first time that Vikram hasn't been a part of my life," I said. "After he left I cried for three days. But I think I'm okay now. I don't know what's going to happen in the future. But right now I want to be here. I'm happy where I am."

I thought back to the look on my father's face when my mother had told him what had happened. His first instinct was to think of Bhushan, his best friend. They had a gentleman's agreement that their children would one day marry. But then my father had glanced at me, seen my puffy eyes and reddened nose, and given me a slight, awkward hug, like he had done on the first day of school.

"Everything will be okay," he had said to me. "Whatever will be will be."

I looked at Toby now.

"Yes," I said. "I think it will all work out."

Toby smiled broadly, that big, beautiful smile.

"I won't be far," he said. "There'll be recitals. You can come. I'd love that."

"I'd love that too," I answered, smiling back.

The September sky was streaked fiery orange. A sudden, sharp breeze that blew inland from the ocean took my breath away. I drew my shawl tightly across my shoulders and ran ahead to catch up with Sangita.

In front of her walked my mother and father, holding hands. We had driven to Santa Barbara for dinner to celebrate our first anniversary in America. Renuka and her parents had joined us. We had raised glasses of club soda and orange juice and clinked them together, laughing. Afterward, on the way home, my father said he wanted to show my mother something.

"This is beautiful," my mother said, standing on the pier. The *pallu* of her sari flapped in the wind. Seagulls squawked overhead. My father took off his jacket and wrapped it around my mother's shoulders. A sailboat was headed back to land. The smell of rusty iron and salty sea lingered in the air.

"It reminds me of something," my mother said.

"Chowpatty beach in Mumbai, with the girls when

246

they were young," my father said.

She nodded in agreement and turned to look at us. Even under her sweater, my sister's arms looked sinewy and muscular. She had made the school swim team. Soon she would compete in regional races.

In my pocket, my phone buzzed, probably Amina again. She and I were on the organizing committee for the Halloween party this year. We were charging an entrance fee. The money was going to help the women in the slums of Calcutta. My father said he would send it personally. Toby was going to be part of the musical lineup. I thought of him now, and a glow lit up my body. I couldn't wait to see him at rehearsal tomorrow.

My mother turned back toward the ocean, leaning over a railing and lifting her face into the wind. Sangita squealed and ran down a flight of rickety steps to the beach. She had seen a fish ejected from the water by a crashing wave. It was flipping and tossing itself on the wet sand, looking for a way to breathe, a way to live. I ran with her and lifted the spinning, silvery fish by its tail. It pirouetted in my hands. I raised it high and, with a gasp of exhilaration and delight, flung it back into its home.

Glossary

beti/beta (bay-tee) – usually used toward someone younger; means "dear/darling"

bhai sahib (bye sahb) – a common way to refer to male acquaintances; literally translates as "brother sir"

bindi (BIHN-dee) – a decorative mark placed in the middle of the forehead by women

chaat (chawt) – platter of savory Indian snacks

chacha (chaw-chaw) – means "father's brother"—a way to differentiate between a maternal and paternal uncle. Chachi is "father's brother's wife."

chai (chy) – traditional Indian spiced tea

chikoo (CHIH-kuu) – popular fruit in India; called sapota in English

choti walli (CHOH-tee WAH-lee) – literally translates as "the girl with the braid"

dada (DAH-dah) – usually used to connote paternal grandfather

dadi (DAH-dee) – usually used to connote paternal grandmother

dals (dawls) – lentils

desi (DEH-see) – reference to people from the Indian subcontinent

dhokla (DOH-kluh) – snack of spicy fermented rice or lentil flour

didi (DEE-dee) – big sister

Diwali (dih-WAH-lee) – Indian New Year

dupatta (duh-PUH-tuh) – long scarf draped over a "salwar kameez" outfit

gopis (GO-pees) – the maidens that the god Krishna danced with in Hindu mythology

jaan (yaHn) – means "life"

jalebis (juh-LAY-bees) – orange-colored dessert shaped like pretzels

jijaji (JEE-juh-jee) – often used to connote "sister's husband"

kaju barfi (KAH-joo BUR-fee) – cashew-nut-based dessert cut into diamond shapes

khandvi (KAHND-vee) – snack made of chickpea flour and yogurt

kohl (kōl) – black eyeliner

ladoos (LUH-doos) – Indian dessert of sweetened chickpea flour rolled into little balls

Limca (LIHM-kuh) – a fizzy lemon drink very popular in India

mangalsutra (mahn-guhl-SOO-truh) – black-and-gold necklace worn by married women

masalas (ma-SAH-las) – spices

mubarak (MOO-bah-ruhk) – congratulations; best wishes

namkaran (NAHM-kah-rahn) – naming ceremony performed by Hindus after the birth of a child

Na roh (Nah ro) – literally translates as "Don't cry"

paan (pawn) – a common food of betel leaf stuffed with a type of tropical nut and other condiments. It is often spat out, leaving a red stain.

pallu (PUH-loo) – part of a sari that drapes across the shoulder

raita (RYE-tuh) – yogurt condiment

salwar kameez (suhl-WAHR ka-MEEZ) – traditional Indian outfit of loose pants and tunic top

shawarma (sha-WER-muh) – Middle Eastern sandwich

sindoor (SIHN-dur) – a red powder worn in the hairline by married women